"The queen of contemporar;

—*BookPage* (starred review)

"Lauren Layne's books are as effervescent and delicious as a brunch mimosa. As soon as you read one, you're going to want another—IMMEDIATELY!"

—Karen Hawkins, *New York Times* bestselling author
of *A Cup of Silver Linings*

"Perfect for readers who love the dishy women's fiction of Candace Bushnell."

—*Booklist*

To Sir, with Love

"Layne crafts a gleefully shameless homage to *Little Shop Around the Corner* and *You've Got Mail* that sparkles like champagne fizz. . . . A delight."

—*Publishers Weekly* (starred review)

"A first-tier purchase."

—*Library Journal* (starred review)

"As light and refreshing as a glass of champagne, *To Sir, with Love* will have you smiling from the first swoon-worthy page to the last."

—Jill Shalvis, *New York Times* bestselling author
of *The Family You Make*

"Breezy dialogue and delightful characters will fully immerse readers in this dreamy and sophisticated love story. . . . A wonderfully satisfying romance."

—*BookPage* (starred review)

"Fans of Nora Ephron will adore this. . . . A charming, witty, heartfelt tale of hope and love and second chances."

—Lori Nelson Spielman, *New York Times* bestselling author
of *The Star-Crossed Sisters of Tuscany*

"Sweet and full of humor . . . readers will be rooting for Gracie to find her Prince Charming."

—*Booklist*

"A charming, swoony, funny, must-read delight of a book!"

—Evie Dunmore, *USA Today* bestselling author of *Portrait of a Scotsman*

"The perfect read while sipping a mai tai on the sand."

—*Cosmopolitan*

"A delight—as sweet and bubbly as a glass of champagne."

—Beth O'Leary, bestselling author of *The Flatshare*

"If you love the 1998 film *You've Got Mail*, you'll love this book."

—*USA Today*

"Crackling with humor and sizzling with romantic tension, this charming modern fairy tale sparkles. I couldn't put it down!"

—Alexis Daria, nationally bestselling author of *A Lot Like Adiós*

"A brilliantly beautiful story that hits all the right spots . . . A definite must-read!"

—*Harlequin Junkie*

PRAISE FOR THE CENTRAL PARK PACT SERIES
Marriage on Madison Avenue

"Breezy and satisfying . . . Sparkling dialogue, hilarious wedding planning scenes, and deeply emotional moments see the series end on a high note."

—*Publishers Weekly*

"Warm and heartfelt, this story conveys author Lauren Layne's real affection for her characters as they overcome the past and build a beautifully messy, perfectly imperfect future."

—*BookPage*

"Irresistibly sweet and funny . . . the heartfelt closure to Lauren Layne's Central Park Pact trilogy that fans have been hoping for."

—*Harlequin Junkie*

Love on Lexington Avenue

"Fans of *Sex and the City* will love this story of finding love where you least expect it."

—*BookBub*

"Simply stunning. Layne's new series is fresh and addictive, and I can't wait for more!"

—Jennifer Probst, *New York Times* bestselling author of *Forever in Cape May*

"These women are so relatable, and you can't help but root for them! If you need a cute romance, look no further."

—*She Reads*

Passion on Park Avenue

"Witty banter and an electric connection between Naomi and Oliver kept me turning the pages late into the night. Lauren Layne knocks this one right out of Park Avenue!"

—Samantha Young, *New York Times* bestselling author of *Much Ado About You*

"Strong characters and relatable situations elevate Layne's bighearted contemporary. . . . [A] vivid enemies-to-lovers romance."

—*Publishers Weekly* (starred review)

"Chic and clever! Like a sexy, comedic movie on the page."

—Tessa Bailey, *New York Times* bestselling author of *It Happened One Summer*

ALSO AVAILABLE FROM LAUREN LAYNE AND GALLERY BOOKS

To Sir, with Love

The Central Park Pact Series
Passion on Park Avenue
Love on Lexington Avenue
Marriage on Madison Avenue

The Wedding Belles Series
From This Day Forward*
To Have and to Hold
For Better or Worse
To Love and to Cherish

---

*ebook only

LAUREN LAYNE

Made in Manhattan

G

GALLERY BOOKS

New York   London   Toronto   Sydney   New Delhi

G

Gallery Books
An Imprint of Simon & Schuster, Inc.
1230 Avenue of the Americas
New York, NY 10020

First Gallery Books trade paperback edition January 2022

GALLERY BOOKS and colophon are registered trademarks of Simon & Schuster, Inc.

For information about special discounts for bulk purchases, please contact Simon & Schuster Special Sales at 1-866-506-1949 or business@simonandschuster.com.

The Simon & Schuster Speakers Bureau can bring authors to your live event. For more information or to book an event, contact the Simon & Schuster Speakers Bureau at 1-866-248-3049 or visit our website at www.simonspeakers.com.

Interior design by Davina Mock-Maniscalco

Manufactured in the United States of America

10 9 8 7 6 5 4 3 2

Library of Congress Cataloging-in-Publication Data
Names: Layne, Lauren, author.
Title: Made in Manhattan / Lauren Layne.
Description: First Gallery Books trade paperback edition. | New York : Gallery Books, 2022.
Identifiers: LCCN 2021033813 (print) | LCCN 2021033814 (ebook) | ISBN 9781982152833 (trade paperback) | ISBN 9781982152840 (ebook)
Classification: LCC PS3612.A9597 M34 2022 (print) | LCC PS3612.A9597 (ebook) | DDC 813/.6—dc23
LC record available at https://lccn.loc.gov/2021033813
LC ebook record available at https://lccn.loc.gov/2021033814

ISBN 978-1-9821-5283-3
ISBN 978-1-9821-5284-0 (ebook)

Made in Manhattan

One

Violet Victoria Townsend was plenty aware that she was the very epitome of a stock character for *snob*.

Ask any sketch artist to draw a pampered Upper East Side princess, and Violet would skip straight to the top of the suspect list. Shiny, bouncy hair? Check. Expertly applied yet barely noticeable makeup? Check. Pretty, but not in the "look again" kind of way? *Yup*.

Her nails were never chipped, her ends never split. Her outfits tended toward neutrals and were always paired with a strand of simple, understated pearls around her neck. Even her home address was eye-rollingly cliché. She'd lived in the same apartment off Madison Avenue since age eleven, when her grandmother took her in.

Did that make Violet a caricature? Perhaps. But a self-aware one. Violet had heard *all* the Blair Waldorf, Charlotte

York, and Holly Golightly comparisons and had made peace with it a long time ago.

So, yeah. She could and often *did* rock a headband. She had a purse dog named after a luxury brand of handbag (Coco, as in Chanel). Did she sometimes summer in the Hamptons? Indeed, and she was guilty of using *summer* as a verb.

But Violet Townsend was also kind to strangers, considerate of others' feelings, and generous with her time. She always brought the perfect hostess gift to a party. Her brunches offered bountiful mimosas with high-quality bacon *and* vegetarian options.

Violet was also heavily involved with a half-dozen charities, volunteered as a tutor every Wednesday afternoon, and was adamantly opposed to gossip, though still somehow found herself knowing everything about everyone.

Not that she expected a medal for any of this. It was just that she figured if she was lucky enough to be born a privileged heiress, she sure as hell better be a good and generous person to go with it.

Which was why, when her late grandmother's best friend had commanded Violet's presence on a Sunday afternoon, Violet hadn't hesitated to reschedule her longstanding Sunday date with *her* best friend.

Edith Rhodes was a precise, specific sort of woman. Violet would know; she'd been serving as Edith's right hand of sorts ever since graduating college. But while Edith was a demanding, high-powered CEO, she was no diva. She planned everything down to the minute, believed that *urgent* was synonymous with *ill-prepared.*

In other words, not the sort of woman to cry wolf. If Edith needed Violet now, it meant *now.* And that something was amiss.

The January afternoon was sunny but brisk as Violet made the short walk to Edith's Park Avenue home. She was perfectly polished as ever, because if Edith had taught Violet anything in the few years since she'd taken her under her wing, it was that emergencies were best approached with lipstick and a great pair of heels.

Violet was dressed in burgundy pumps, gray slacks, a white blouse, and, of course, the ever-present pearls that had become her trademark of sorts, even if their legacy was a bit sad.

But Violet didn't like to think about that.

"Good afternoon, Alvin," she said, stepping into the foyer and smiling at Edith's live-in butler, maintenance man, and all-around loyal companion.

He looked pointedly at Violet's feet, where Coco was usually happily prancing around her ankles. "And where is my little lady?"

"At home, getting her beauty sleep. She hates the cold, and her best sweaters are dirty," she said with a wink, though her little Yorkie really *did* have a pile of doggy-sized sweaters in Violet's laundry basket.

She gave Alvin an assessing once-over. "How are we today?"

He took her jacket with one hand and patted his slightly rounded belly with the other, looking forlorn. "It's the stomach, dear. Probably an ulcer. Could be much worse."

"Mmm." She made a sympathetic noise, even as she tucked her tongue into her cheek. "I'm so sorry to hear that. What did Dr. Howell say?"

He frowned at her, looking just the slightest bit sulky, closer to six than his actual sixty.

Violet waited. Patient.

His frown deepened a little as he huffed, relenting. "Gas," he admitted. "But the doctor seemed off his game. I may go back in a week when he's got his head on straight."

"Of course," Violet said. She pointed at his foot. "And the toe?"

Last week, Alvin had self-diagnosed a sore toe as gangrene, for which amputation was the only likely cure, even as Edith had reminded him he'd stubbed that very toe on the sideboard in the dining room.

He blinked, no doubt struggling to keep track of his many ailments, then a little sheepishly said, "Oh. The toe's better."

"Wonderful." Violet smiled. "I'm glad you got to keep it after all."

He narrowed his eyes, then waggled a scolding finger at her. "When you were little, you didn't used to sass me."

"Who's sassing?" she asked innocently, kissing his cheek as she moved toward the parlor. He was an exhausting hypochondriac, but he was *her* hypochondriac. "Edith in here?"

"Yes." Alvin's playful demeanor evaporated, replaced with concern, and not for his ulcer/gas.

The door was open a crack, and Edith's head snapped up when Violet stepped into the room.

"Violet." Edith's utterance was more breath than word, and Violet's stomach lurched in worry. The Edith she knew was never rattled, but the woman in front of her now looked downright fragile.

Edith seemed to sense Violet's thoughts, because she resolutely straightened her shoulders.

"Where's Coco?" Edith asked with a frown, glancing around the floor where Violet's dog generally ran in circles.

"Home," Violet said, sitting beside Edith on the love seat, taking her hand, and getting straight to the point. "What's wrong?"

Edith swallowed, her free hand lifting to fiddle with her necklace. Violet's concern notched up to outright alarm. Edith Rhodes did *not* fiddle.

The older woman slowly, deliberately dropped her hand back into her lap, as though trying to regain control. "It's about Adam."

Violet squeezed Edith's hand in silent sympathy. Edith's only son had died just a few months earlier. The loss had been hard on Edith, obviously, but Violet suspected that even

Edith knew she'd lost Adam to addiction and his hard-partying ways long before he'd overdosed on a toxic mix of alcohol and heroin.

Which was why Edith's distress *now* was a bit puzzling. A delayed reaction, perhaps, though Edith didn't seem the type. She dealt with everything in the here and now.

Edith swallowed, then cleared her throat, her eyes darting nervously to the far corner of the room, before coming back to Violet. "You know that Bernard and I hoped to leave the company to Adam."

Violet nodded, carefully hiding her skepticism about how *that* would have gone. The Adam Rhodes that Violet had known had been in no condition to take over a lemonade stand, much less the Rhodes International conglomerate. Violet wasn't technically an employee herself, but as Edith's right hand and personal assistant for several years, she'd learned enough about the business to know that multimillion-dollar real estate investment deals were on the table daily; not exactly the place for a man whose primary concern at work had been keeping his corner office sideboard stocked with his beloved bourbon.

"Knowing that Rhodes would pass out of the family made Adam's passing doubly hard," Edith continued, swallowing. "I should have made peace with it long ago, with Adam being who he was, and an only child who never married . . ."

Violet nodded again, this time in understanding. Edith

had lost a beloved husband just last year, then a son months later. Since Violet had lost, well, *everyone*, she knew all too well the ache, the sense of being unmoored with nothing—and no one—to hold on to. "What can I do? What do you need?"

Edith's blue gaze searched Violet's face affectionately. "You've always been so good to me."

Violet gave her a gently reprimanding look. "Says the woman who helped raise me. You're practically family. Tell me what's bothering you. We'll fix it."

Edith's fingers went to her temples, past the point of pretending she was fine. "It's no secret Adam was always a bit wild."

Understatement. "Sure."

"Well, it would seem he had one *particularly* wild escapade during spring break his junior year of college. He went to . . . Cabo . . . Cancún . . . I forget," Edith said with a wave of her hand. "He met a girl, and, well, you know Adam. He always liked women."

Lots of women, Violet mentally amended.

"Is there . . . is this woman threatening blackmail of some kind?" Violet asked, trying to keep from begging Edith to spit it out already.

"She's dead."

Violet jolted, because the cold pronouncement hadn't come from Edith, but from a harsh, masculine voice behind them.

Violet stood, the smooth motion belying her galloping heart as she searched for the source of the voice.

She stilled when she saw the man leaning against the mantel at the far side of the room. How in the world she had missed him when she'd entered was beyond her. Violet couldn't make out much of him from his place lurking in the shadows, but his sheer *presence* seemed enormous. Looming and very *male*, especially when contrasted with the fussy Victorian decor of Edith Rhodes's parlor.

For that matter, this man didn't even look as though he knew what a parlor was. He was dressed in faded jeans, a long-sleeved T-shirt, and scuffed boots, and one thing was abundantly clear: he did not belong here.

"Get out," Violet said, taking calm command of the situation. "I don't know who you are, but you can't just come barging in like some sort of . . . some sort of—"

A very dark eyebrow lifted in insolent challenge. *Some sort of what?*

"Violet." Edith's voice was quiet.

Violet meant to look at the other woman, but she seemed to be locked in the angry, sullen gaze of the stranger.

"Violet," Edith said, her voice a bit more steady this time. "I'd like to introduce you to my long-lost grandson."

Two

The silence went off like a rocket, explosive and all-consuming in its stillness.

Grandson!

Edith didn't have a grandson. Adam was an only child, had never married, had never had children—

Violet's brain slowly caught up as she recalled what Edith had just told her about Adam's "wild" spring break. It had clearly resulted in . . .

Him. The man leaning against the mantel hadn't moved a muscle.

Violet blinked rapidly, trying to regain her composure. Tried, and failed, because the next words out of her mouth were atypically rude. "Are you sure?"

"This is Cain Rhodes," Edith said, her tone leaving no room for doubt. "Adam's son."

"Stone," he snapped.

The single word, harshly uttered, rippled through Violet with unsettling intensity. He had a rasp of a voice: low, angry, and . . . southern? It certainly wasn't the crisp tones she was used to hearing from men in her social circle.

"Stone?" Violet repeated.

He dipped his chin downward. "My name is Cain Stone. Not *Rhodes*." He practically spat the last word as though it was an obscenity.

Cain Stone.

She repeated his name in her head, decided it was fitting. It had a sharp brusqueness to it, which certainly fit its owner.

Edith stood, and Violet instinctively reached out to keep her steady. But Edith gave her a sharp look, and Violet dropped her hand, knowing Edith's dislike for demonstrations of weakness.

Edith nodded toward her grandson. "When Adam was in college, Cain's mother and Adam had a—"

"They fucked," Cain said in a bored tone.

If he was going for shock value, he succeeded in surprising Violet, but Edith merely shot him a cool, disapproving look. "Cain was the product of their union."

Violet pressed her lips together, torn between amusement and alarm. The contrast between grandmother's and grandson's word choice could not be more telling.

"How did he find you?" Violet asked Edith, trying to pretend that Cain's intensely masculine presence didn't unnerve her.

He picked up on the skepticism in Violet's tone and gave an incredulous laugh. "You think I'm a fraud?"

Actually, *yes*. Violet did think that. She lifted her chin and met his eyes to let him know it.

There was no way this rough, ill-mannered man had Rhodes blood running through his veins. Adam Rhodes may have been a dedicated party boy, but he'd had blue blood through and through, polished to the point of slickness. Violet found it hard to fathom that Adam could have fathered someone so . . . *coarse*.

"Listen, Duchess," Cain said mockingly, pushing away from the mantel and standing to his full height, which was . . . tall. Very tall. "Her majesty here came and found *me*, so you can take all your suspicious snobbery and shove it right up your tight little—"

"He's quite right," Edith interrupted quickly. "I sought him out. Not the other way around."

"Why didn't you tell me?" Violet asked softly, trying to hide her hurt. Edith was as close to family as Violet had, and she'd thought the sentiment went both ways. Just in the past few weeks, they'd celebrated Christmas Eve, Christmas Day, and New Year's together.

Holidays and personal relationship aside, they'd also

spent countless weekday hours together, Edith as the CEO of Rhodes International, Violet as her right hand. There'd been more than enough opportunity for Edith to bring Violet up to speed on something this momentous, she'd just . . .

Chosen not to.

The appearance of a *grandson* was easily the biggest event in Edith's life since her husband's and son's passing, and yet somehow, Violet hadn't made it onto her list of confidants.

Violet inhaled, trying to tuck the pain away to be unpacked later, but her tone was still accusatory. "How long have you known?"

"Just after Thanksgiving, I finally forced myself to go through some of Adam's things. There was a birth certificate. Eve Stone was the mother, Adam unmistakably listed as the father. And a baby boy. Cain."

A flicker of amusement edged out some of Violet's hurt, and she lifted three fingers to her lips in an unsuccessful attempt to hold back a laugh. "Adam and Eve had a baby, and they named him Cain? As in Cain and Abel?"

"*She,*" the man corrected in a low warning tone. "My *mother* named me. Adam didn't have shit to do with it."

"Fine," Violet said in a reasonable tone, shifting to face him. "So your *mother* named you after an Old Testament murderer who committed fratricide?"

He merely glared at her.

"Fratricide refers to the killing of one's broth—"

"I know what it means," he snapped. "And I don't have a brother, dead or otherwise."

"You *do* have a grandmother, however," Edith interjected, bringing them back to the point at hand. "Which makes you the only heir to Rhodes International."

Violet prided herself in tidily hiding her emotions, but even her carefully practiced self-control had limits, and her mouth dropped open. "*Edith*. You cannot be serious. You want to turn over the company?"

She managed to withhold the incredulous addition of "to *him*?"

Barely.

"He's my grandson," Edith repeated, as though she needed to keep reminding herself of that fact. "The company has always been run by a Rhodes. And it was Bernard's dying wish that it stay that way."

"But Bernard couldn't have known Adam would die so tragically young, or that his only son . . ."

Violet cast Cain a dubious glance, and he narrowed his eyes in response.

Edith's gaze was pleading as she stared at Violet, begging her to understand. "He's family."

"*Family*," the man echoed tauntingly. "I don't know how things work in this concrete monstrosity you call a city, or this museum you call home, but where I'm from, *family* doesn't pretend someone doesn't exist for thirty years."

"Oh, would you quit squawking about that," Edith said impatiently. Violet bit back a smile. "I'll say this one last time until you get it through your head: there was no pretending. I didn't know you existed until recently, and I began seeking you out the very *second* I found out."

Cain snorted in derision. "Meaning you got out your checkbook and sent someone to Louisiana to come find me."

Louisiana. That explained the accent.

Edith clasped her hands and gave him a pleading look that Violet had never seen before. "Cain, please. I was skeptical . . . I didn't think Adam would have kept my only grandson from me—"

"Dear old Dad sounds like a real asshole," Cain drawled.

"Like father like son," Violet said under her breath.

Edith's hearing wasn't as good as it once was, and she missed Violet's remark.

Cain had not.

His dark eyes cut over to her, darkening in annoyance before returning his attention to his grandmother. "I told you, I don't want any part of this."

"And yet, you're here," Edith said just a bit smugly.

He crossed his arms and scowled. "Can't say the words *billion-dollar company* didn't have me curious. But I don't belong here."

"No, you don't," Edith said bluntly. "Which is why I've asked Violet to join us."

Violet jolted at the mention of her name. She'd been assuming Edith had called her here for moral support, but seeing the stubborn, speculative expression on Edith's face had Violet bracing for a more taxing request.

"My retirement at the end of the year's a foregone conclusion," Edith said. "The board is already planning to vote for my replacement. And though I'd resigned myself to handing over the reins to a non-Rhodes, if I don't *have* to . . ."

The raw hope in Edith's voice scraped at Violet's heart.

"I can teach him to run the company," Edith said to Violet with almost girlish enthusiasm. "It'll be a steep learning curve, but it can be done. The boy's sharp."

Violet's lips twitched as the large, angry man let out a slight growl at being described as a *boy*.

"But those rough edges will need smoothing," Edith continued, not bothering to lower her voice. "He'll need an entrée not just into the business world, which I can offer, but into the social circle—*your* social circle."

"Now hold on," Cain interrupted angrily. "I have no intention of getting anywhere near the duchess and her fellow Barbies. She looks more like the woman on an ugly broach my mom inherited from my grandma—my *real* grandma—than she does a real woman."

Violet bristled. It was one thing to insult her, but his words had been chosen to deliberately wound Edith, and that was *not* okay with her.

"Well then, feel free to hightail it on back to Louisiana," Violet snapped with uncharacteristic temper. "Because I can assure you the *broach* and her Barbies don't want anything to do with your torn-up jeans and ponytail."

"Violet." Edith's voice was openly pleading now, and Violet looked at her warily.

"Please. Teach him. Help him belong."

Violet and Cain let out twin laughs—his rougher than hers, but no less derisive.

"You're joking," Violet said just as Cain snarled a "*Hell no.*"

Edith scowled at them as though they were rebellious children. "It's a logical plan. Nobody knows the unspoken rules of Manhattan life like Violet."

Violet flinched. She knew Edith had meant it as a compliment, but for the briefest of moments, her heart sank at the thought that that was perhaps *all* she was. A collection of rules. Rules she never questioned, always followed. A vessel for pretty manners, problem solving, and whatever anyone needed from her.

Edith was too distracted to catch Violet's wince, but she saw from the way Cain's gaze sharpened in assessment that he'd seen her reaction and made note of it.

So he was observant. Which boded well for him assimilating into New York life—

No. *No!* She wasn't seriously considering this.

Was she?

It was an impossible task. And yet . . .

Impossible was strangely appealing. How long since she had challenged herself? In anything?

Or since someone—even Edith—had thought her capable of anything beyond sitting still, looking pretty, and taking care of the seating arrangements.

Could she take this angry, uncouth man and turn him into someone who held his own in a boardroom? Who could navigate the sticky intricacies of the New York social set?

Who could not only tie a tie, but look good in it?

Suddenly she wanted to try, rather desperately.

But Violet was also increasingly aware that Edith had made a rare error in judgment. She seemed to be under the impression that it was *Violet* who needed convincing. Perhaps because of her emotional attachment to the idea of family, Edith didn't seem to realize that it was Cain himself who would be the biggest obstacle to her grand plan. It took only one look at the angry set of his jaw to know he was itching to take the first flight back to Louisiana.

If he stayed, it wouldn't be because of family loyalty. Judging from the look on his face, even the promise of money and prestige might not be enough. He was ready to bolt.

But maybe, just maybe, if Violet could hit at his *pride* . . .

"It'd just be a wardrobe overhaul," Edith was saying, having regained her composure. "A few lessons in decorum. Show him around town, introduce him to people his own age."

Cain spread his hands to the side. "Hate to tell you, Granny, but I can run your precious company just fine in what I'm wearing."

Violet let out a delighted, condescending laugh, deliberately crafted to goad him. "Are you certain? Because it looks to me like you could start chewing on hay any moment."

"Bet hay would be right good to scoop up caviar," he said, exaggerating his drawl.

Violet extended her hand, palm up, and gave Edith a telling look. *You see?*

"You're asking the impossible," Violet said with a sad shake of her head, as though regretful. "I'd be happy to show him around town, but as long as he's scared to death of failing . . ."

Cain gave an incredulous laugh. "Scared? What the fuck?"

Violet looked at him with wide, innocent eyes. "You shouldn't be embarrassed. It's a monumental task she's asking of you, and I understand completely if you're not up to it."

"Oh, you understand completely," he repeated in a mocking, uppity tone. His eyebrow arched upward in derision. "Reverse psychology, Duchess? That was your big plan?"

Violet inspected her nails to avoid having to confirm that he was exactly right. It had been worth a shot.

Cain shook his head at Edith with a contemptuous smirk. "You brought in the wrong girl, Edith. Duchess here is in over her head and doesn't have the backbone to deal with anything outside of her comfort zone. She'd quit before the first week of trying to turn me into your puppet."

Violet moved toward Cain for the first time, stepping between him and Edith so he was forced to address her directly. "Prove it."

"I already told you, those mind games won't—"

"I think you're right, this won't last a week," she spoke over him. "But it won't be me who backs out—it'll be *you* who realizes you're out of your league. You won't last a day in my world."

His eyes seemed to spark, if only briefly, at the challenge, and his jaw worked in clenched tension as though warring with his own instincts.

Then he swore, a low, long string of curses, half of which Violet had never even heard.

"Fine," he snapped at his grandmother. "If Duchess here wants to play dress-up, I'll be her doll if it means I inherit a fucking fortune."

"*Wonderful,*" Edith said, clapping her hands in delight and ignoring her grandson's profanity and clear disdain for the situation. "I'll just go tell Alvin to bring in some champagne."

Edith swept out of the room, her typical younger-than-her-age vitality restored, and the moment she was gone, Violet allowed her sweetly demure smile to widen in smug triumph.

"You're pleased with yourself," Cain said in a bored voice as he ambled toward her. He was even taller than she realized, and broader too. Once again, the unfamiliar, untamed masculinity made her heartbeat a little too fast, her breath a bit ragged. "Think you've handled me, have you?"

Since she guessed his proximity was deliberately meant to make her ill at ease, Violet forced herself to lift her face all the way to his and meet his gaze dead-on.

It was a mistake.

Up close, she could see his lashes were thick and curled with surprising gold tips. Up close, he smelled like mint and soap, without any hint of cologne.

It was irritatingly appealing.

Cain's gaze was doing some exploring of its own, his eyes taking their time, starting at her hairline and moving— slowly—all the way down to her feet, as though seeing her *truly* for the first time.

When his eyes snapped back to hers, she felt a pull low in her stomach. *Uh-oh.*

"Haven't I?" Violet said, relieved her voice wasn't as breathless as she felt. "Handled you?"

His smile was slow. Predatory. He moved even closer until she could feel his body heat. "Careful, Duchess. Look at me that way again, and you'll be the one who's *handled*, and not the least bit gently."

She sucked in a breath at the unapologetically sexual undertone.

"Don't worry," Cain murmured mockingly. "I guarantee you'll like it."

Three

"You've *got* to be joking."

Since it was the third time Keith had uttered that very statement, Violet didn't hurry to respond. She cut off a bite-size piece of scallop and dragged it through the decadent butter sauce. She set the scallop on her tongue, savoring the richness for just a moment before chewing, swallowing, and taking a sip of chardonnay.

Finally, she looked back at Keith. "I'm not joking. Would it help to sink in if I wrote it down for you?"

Keith blinked in surprise at the sharpness in her tone, and Violet couldn't blame him. She rarely resorted to waspishness, but ever since her meeting with Edith and her newly discovered grandson yesterday, she'd felt out of sorts.

She'd picked up her phone a half-dozen times to tell Edith she couldn't do it. Or rather, that she didn't *want* to do it—didn't want to spend the foreseeable future with a man who clearly couldn't stand her.

But every time, Violet had set the phone back down again. Partially because she hated the thought of disappointing Edith, but mostly because it felt like letting Cain win.

The man had made it clear he didn't think she'd survive a week in his company. The last thing she wanted to do was let him think that she was so meek and sheltered as to back down before they'd even begun, especially given the taunting way he'd ended the conversation. She wouldn't give him the satisfaction of knowing how much he'd rattled her. Or that in that moment, she'd forgotten that Keith even existed.

She was on edge, yes, but also determined, which was odd in itself. Violet wasn't the sort to make a point for the sake of making a point. She was good at smoothing ruffled feathers, problem solving, and supporting people. That she was motivated to take on Cain Stone out of pride and dislike was out of character.

Violet looked across the table, caught Keith's nonplussed expression, and realized she'd better put her feather-smoothing skills to work.

Violet smiled and reached for Keith's hand. He glanced at it, hesitating a moment before covering her hand with his. The touch was warm and familiar, if not exactly electric.

She'd made peace with their lack of chemistry long ago.

As far as Violet was concerned, there were more important things than butterflies and passion. She wanted someone who would be there for her, someone she could count on.

Keith was steady.

Safe.

Not the sexiest of adjectives, but it was important to her nonetheless. Violet had lost her parents at a young age and had been taken in by her grandmother. Years later, in college, her support network had been obliterated once again when she'd been dumped by her longtime boyfriend in the same year she'd lost her grandma.

Knowing that loss was inevitable had led Violet to seek out safety wherever she could, for as long as she could have it. It was part of why she appreciated Edith's stalwart dependability, even if the woman could be less than warm. It had also impacted Violet's romantic priorities. Her college boyfriend had been fun, and passionate, and spontaneous; she'd adored him, which had made it all the more crushing when his spontaneity had resulted in him falling in love with someone else and leaving Violet without ceremony.

These days, she treaded a bit more carefully and prized a different set of qualities. She wanted a man who was dependable and safe.

A man like Keith.

It didn't hurt that she and Keith had always felt a little inevitable, almost as though they'd been tailor-made for each other. They'd grown up in the same neighborhood, they'd gone to the same school, and their parents had attended the same functions.

Not that they'd been friends, at least, not exactly. Four years her senior, Keith had mostly been the handsome older boy she and her girlfriends had giggled over at family friendly holiday parties.

For his part, he'd barely known she existed.

All of that changed in college when Violet had suddenly lost her grandma, and no longer had the boyfriend she'd come to lean on to get her through it.

Lonely and hurting, Violet had gratefully let herself be taken under Edith's wing, and it had been at one of Edith's many parties that Violet and Keith's paths crossed again. They'd been friendly, but at that first meeting, he'd had a date. The second time they'd met, *she'd* been with someone. This had gone on for a year or two until they'd finally gotten their timing right and shown up to a New Year's Eve party solo. A midnight kiss had turned into a Valentine's Day dinner, then a Labor Day gathering in Southampton, and now here they were.

Her twenty-seven, him thirty-one, and . . . together?

In truth, Violet never knew what to call Keith. *Boyfriend* felt juvenile and fluttery. They weren't engaged, and *lovers* didn't apply—not for months now. She supposed they were partners, though she'd be hard-pressed to define what they were partners in.

Mostly, Violet reassured herself that theirs was the sort

of grown-up, adult relationship that didn't require labels or promises. They enjoyed the same restaurants. They frequently attended dinner parties together and were each other's usual companions to nights at the orchestra and black-tie fundraisers. Keith's parents adored her, and when Violet had dinner at Edith's, it was taken for granted that Keith would join more often than not.

Violet knew everyone assumed they were headed for marriage. She was less clear on how she felt about that.

"Have you actually met this Cain?" Keith asked, apparently mollified by her soothing. "Edith brought him by the office, and he's . . ." Keith waved his free hand. "God, I don't even have the words."

Trying to stifle her irritation at his relentless griping about the Cain topic, she pulled her hand back and picked up her knife and fork once more. "Yes, I've met him."

"The maintenance man fixing the thermostat was better dressed."

Violet sucked in her cheeks. His condescension rankled, mostly because it was an uncomfortable mirror to her own thoughts, her own snobbery.

"Easily fixed," Violet said calmly. "I'll take him to get some suits."

Keith snorted. "You know as well as I do that it takes more than Edith's credit card and a good tailor to make him look the part."

"Keith," she said, both chiding and soothing.

"Sorry," he muttered, adjusting his tie as though it were choking him. "It just . . . it pisses me off that a hobo in a pony-tail who's never even met a razor can come in and take what the rest of us have actually worked for."

Ah. So *that* was the reason for his extra prickliness: pro-fessional resentment.

Keith was a senior vice president at Rhodes, *and* he sat on the board. His job meant everything to him, and Edith always seemed pleased with his performance, even going so far as to say in admiration that he'd climbed the ladder faster than anyone she'd known.

If Cain took over as CEO, he'd make Keith's rate of as-cension up the ranks decidedly less impressive.

"I imagine that's a difficult pill to swallow," Violet said. "But it's not like you didn't know it was coming. Rhodes has always been a family company, and everyone knows the only reason Edith stayed on long past standard retirement age was because she was waiting for Adam to get his act together."

He said nothing.

"Keith?" she prompted.

He took a distracted bite of his dinner and shrugged. "That felt different. Everyone knew Adam would never be sober enough to run the company. It was only going to be a matter of time until Edith realized she'd have to turn over the reins to someone else."

Violet's eyebrows lifted. "Does *Edith* know that?"

He made an impatient noise. "You know how she is.

Stubborn and set in her ways and obsessed with her family's 'legacy.' It's always pissed her off that sheer force of personality couldn't manufacture bloodlines."

"Which is probably why she was so excited to learn about her grandson," Violet pointed out. "It's a Hail Mary chance at preserving the Rhodes legacy after all."

He rolled his eyes. "I forgot how blindly loyal you are to that woman."

"Loyal, yes," Violet said, trying to keep the edge out of her voice. "But not blind. Edith's done a lot for me over the years. *And* for you, I might add. She hired you to a senior position before you were even thirty."

"Because I was qualified."

Or because I asked her to, Violet added silently.

"I'm happy for Edith," Violet said truthfully. "She deserves to have the opportunity to keep the company in the family."

Keith pinched the bridge of his nose. "This isn't an episode of *Dynasty*, Violet. CEO titles aren't inherited anymore."

"Okay, fine," she said, realizing he wouldn't change the subject until he got whatever he needed to off his chest. "Who do *you* think should take over the company?"

Keith shrugged and took another bite of duck.

She tilted her head and studied him. "You?"

He put his fork aside with calm precision. "Why *not* me? I'm as close to family as she's got."

Violet blinked in puzzlement. "How do you figure?"

"Well, you're *practically* her granddaughter. And you and I are . . ."

He waved his hand, as though to say it was obvious.

You and I are what?

Suddenly, Violet wanted very much for him to finish that sentence, as an alarming thought popped into her head: What if her personal connection to the CEO of Rhodes International was why Keith had persistently courted her despite their lack of chemistry?

What if . . .

No. Violet pushed the uncomfortable, unflattering thought aside. She and Keith were an item well *before* he joined Rhodes. And there was nothing wrong with professional ambition. He was good at his job, even Edith had said as much. Why *shouldn't* he have his eye on the top spot of any company?

Keith winced. "God. I'm sorry. I sound like an ass. It's just that I care about Edith too, Violet."

Violet instantly softened, feeling guilty for her traitorous thoughts.

Keith continued. "I can't stand the thought of some money-grabbing outsider taking advantage just because his mom happened to get knocked up by Edith's son."

Annnnnd, just like that, her warm thoughts evaporated.

"How delicately put, Keith," Violet murmured. "And for what it's worth, from what I've seen, Cain isn't exactly beating on the door of the corner office. I'm not even sure he wants to be here."

"Yeah, I'm sure having a company and a billion dollars handed to him is a real tough pill to swallow," he said sarcastically into his glass of wine.

"You're getting ahead of yourself," Violet said. "Regardless of Edith's wishes, the board still has to vote him in."

Keith looked at her, then seemed to relax for the first time all night. "You're right. You're right, of course. The board is loyal to Edith, but not to the point of insanity. They'll see him for what he is."

"And what's that?" she asked curiously.

Keith lifted a shoulder, digging into his meal with enthusiasm now. "He's not one of us, Vi."

"Not yet," she said. "But once I'm through with him . . ."

He let out a little laugh of disbelief that chafed at her already raw nerves. "You really think you can do it? Get him to fit in?"

She picked up her wineglass and lifted it in a toast with a small smile. "Watch me."

Four

The day after her lunch with Keith, Violet stood in front of the late Adam Rhodes's brownstone, preparing to *My Fair Lady* the heck out of his reluctant son.

She tilted her head back to look at the skinny, three-story building as she absently reached into her bag and scratched Coco's head. It wasn't that she'd specifically *wanted* a dog that fit into her purse. It was more that she'd fallen in love with a dog that had turned out to be just three pounds fully grown and was one tiny, lazy diva.

"You remember this place, sweetie?" she asked the dog. "You took a twosie in the entryway when you were a puppy."

The dog gave her a baleful look. *Mom. Really?*

"Our secret. Nobody but us knows," Violet reassured her, rubbing a thumb over a silky ear. She didn't tell the dog that the reason nobody but them knew was that Adam and his dinner party guests had been several martinis in at the time, not to mention whatever other substances had made an appearance that night.

Violet thought of the man who lived there now and pursed her lips. Unlike his wastrel father, he didn't seem the type to relish going through life being completely out of it. In fact, she sensed Cain saw plenty. Too much.

Coco ducked back into the purse, spinning in three tight circles, before curling into a sleepy ball.

Taking a deep breath, Violet made her way up the stairs, stepping carefully in her high heels, since the concrete was cracked and desperately in need of repairs.

She'd been to the home plenty of times over the years. Adam, despite his many, *many* flaws, had been Edith's son. And since Edith was practically family, that made Adam family. During his too-few sober periods, he'd even acted as a father figure to her. He hadn't been clean often, but Violet had cherished the moments when he was. Adam had been one of her father's best friends and his best man at her parents' wedding.

When Violet's grandmother had been alive, she was always eager to regale Violet with stories of her parents. But even as a teenager, Violet had sensed her grandmother's stories were candy coated, either because of the natural bias of a mother's affection for her son and daughter-in-law, or in an effort to portray David and Lisa Townsend in the best possible light for their daughter.

Adam's version of David and Lisa, on the other hand, had felt more vibrant and real. Violet had cherished the rare moments he'd been sober enough to humor her eager questions about her family. Adam's stories had portrayed Violet's father as a man full of mischief, with a wicked sense of humor and an itch to see the world beyond the pristine one he'd been born into.

As Violet had gotten older, she'd surmised that that itch must have been what brought Adam and her father together as best friends in the first place. Both men, in their way, had been seeking refuge from their straitlaced upbringing.

Adam, in drugs and alcohol.

Violet's father, in his need for adventure, the farther from NYC, the better.

In both cases, the men's respective lifestyle choices had ultimately led to their demise. Violet also wondered if they'd ever regretted those choices, or taken a moment to see the effect their lifestyle had on those around them. Had Adam or her father ever sensed that "fun-loving" also had a dark side? That it left the people who loved them horribly, achingly *alone*?

Violet consciously pushed the melancholy thoughts aside and refocused her attention on a man who was even more of a mystery to her than her late father or his flawed best friend.

A man whom she had less than two months to turn from an angry, ponytailed Louisiana resident into a Park Avenue–approved, boardroom-ready executive.

She had no illusions that it was going to be easy. She wasn't even sure it was *possible*.

But she'd come armed with at least one weapon: the element of surprise.

Edith had given Violet Cain's cell number, and she purposely hadn't used it. If she was going to figure out how to change Cain, she needed to know what made him tick. And if she was going to do that, she needed to get a glimpse of the real man, before he had time to put up his walls.

There was, of course, every chance he'd ignore her or that he wasn't even home, which led her to the second advantage, and it was a big one: she had the keys to Adam's brownstone.

Cain's father had given them to her for emergencies, and as far as Violet was concerned, this whole mess she'd agreed to definitely qualified. Still, she supposed the man deserved some semblance of warning, so Violet knocked rather than immediately letting herself in.

Ignoring the old-fashioned door knocker, she gave a pert rap to the door with her knuckles. Coco popped her head back out of the bag to investigate, but she was the only one. Cain either hadn't heard the knock or was pretending not to.

Violet knocked again, more firmly this time. Still nothing. She shifted subtly to her left so she could look through the paned window.

She waited. And waited some more.

Her eyes narrowed; she was almost positive that she saw

a blurry shadow of movement inside and heard the sound of footsteps, but still, the door didn't open.

"All right, Mr. Stone, we'll do this your way," she muttered. "Mannerless and crude it is."

Violet reached into her purse, Coco sneaking in a series of doggie kisses as her fingers searched for the key.

Finding it, she stuck the key into the dead bolt and was just twisting the handle when the front door swung open, pulling her forward with such force that she slammed into a wall.

But the wall was a *man*. A bare-chested man.

Startled, Violet's free hand found the center of his chest as she pushed backward, only she overdid it and teetered on her stilettos.

Cain reached out to steady her, his hands warm against her upper arms, even as he scowled down at her.

Once she was steady on her feet, he released her as though she burned him. "What sort of idiotic shoes are those? And what the *hell* are you doing at my house, Viola?"

She gave him a withering look, because she didn't think for one second he didn't remember her name, and he knew *exactly* what she was doing here.

He crossed his arms, and even as they engaged in a staring contest, the details of their situation began to creep into Violet's consciousness. The man was not only shirtless, but his jeans were very much *unbuttoned*, as though they'd been slung on in a hurry.

She chewed the inside of her cheek. "Button your pants."

"It's my house. Get out if you don't like how I'm dressed."

"*Un*dressed," she clarified.

Coco made her presence known to Cain for the first time, letting out a bark as though backing up her mistress's assertion.

Cain's gaze dropped to her bag, horrified. "What is that?"

She rolled her eyes. "It's a dog."

His scowl was skeptical. "In what world, Oz?"

Coco made a whining noise, and Violet frowned at Cain as she pointed at the little Yorkie. "You hurt her feelings."

"I'm already exhausted by all the sleep I'll lose tonight over that fact."

Violet exhaled for patience. "New York manners dictate that you invite me in."

"Manners *everywhere* dictate that you shouldn't break into someone else's house."

"Touché and agreed. Perhaps you're not a lost cause after all. But it's cold out here, so . . ." Violet stepped inside, careful not to touch him as she scooted into the foyer.

"Also, isn't it a bit soon to be calling it *your* house?" she said. "You've been here, what, a week?"

"A week too long," he grumbled, shutting the front door.

She glanced his way. "You don't like the place?"

Adam hadn't done much with the outside of the brownstone, preferring to leave it to its timeless, stately appearance that the Upper East Side legacies liked to call classic but sometimes just translated to *old*. Inside, however, the man had spared no expense renovating it with modern amenities.

Unlike Edith's and Violet's homes, which had been deliberately decorated to preserve the prewar aesthetic, Adam had leaned into the twenty-first century. As far as Violet knew, the hardwood floors were just about the only thing original in the home. Adam had skipped right over contemporary and gone straight to *modern*.

Adam had spared no cost in letting his interior designer go wild, but for all the expense, Violet had always disliked the place. Everything from the white giraffe hat rack to the neon-orange modular sofa gave her an overall sense of discomfort.

The cool, ultra-mod vibe had fit Adam's slick personality and modern playboy persona perfectly, but Violet couldn't help but notice how out of place his son seemed in the environment. Very bull in china shop.

Cain followed her into the kitchen, frown firmly in place as he confirmed her observations. "Hell no, I don't like the place."

Violet looked around for coffee, but the counters were mostly bare, save for a pizza box.

"You don't drink coffee?" she asked, setting her bag on the floor so that Coco had the option to hop out and explore if she wanted.

He leaned on the counter, either not noticing or not

caring that he was still only half dressed. "I do. But there's no coffeepot."

Violet opened the cupboard to the right of the sink. As she'd hoped, Adam's French press was still there, and there was even a bag of unopened coffee beans. The coffee was a bit past its prime, certainly, but at least it was caffeine; Violet was feeling increasingly weary and they'd barely gotten started.

She set about making the coffee, sensing Cain's gaze tracking her every movement.

"Come here often, do ya?" Cain asked sarcastically as Violet dumped beans into the grinder she found in one of the lower cabinets.

She shrugged. "I knew your father well."

"How well?"

She gave him a wary look out of the corner of her eye as she put the kettle on to heat the water. "He was a family friend."

"*Friend*, as in . . ." He waggled his eyebrows, deliberately crude.

Violet didn't bother dignifying that with a response. "How do you take your coffee?"

"Black." He nodded at the French press. "What the hell is that?"

"It's a French press. A type of coffeepot."

"Looks like a pain in the ass," he said, straightening and lifting his arms over his head to stretch.

"Sorry it's not instant," she said just a little snidely.

He surprised her by laughing, a low rumble. "Damn, you really are a snob."

"I'm not," she said automatically.

His snort said it all.

"So," she said as she set a timer for four minutes and turned to face him. "Since we're stuck with each other, we might as well get to know the basics. Tell me about Cain Stone."

"You've got to be kidding me," he said, one eye on her purse as Coco hopped out of the bag and began sniffing the hardwood floor in earnest. Cain's attention came back to Violet. "You barge into my house at the crack of dawn, and you think we're going to make small talk?"

Violet blinked. "The crack of dawn? It's ten thirty in the morning."

He shook his head. "Clearly, you've never been to N'awlins. This is very much morning."

"You lived there your whole life?" she asked, jumping at the opening to know him better. To *understand* him. For Edith's sake, of course.

"No."

Before she could press him to elaborate, the unmistakable sound of bare feet on wood steps caught her attention.

She looked at Cain, startled to learn they weren't alone in the house. He didn't look the least bit surprised when a short, curvy blonde padded into the kitchen wearing nothing but bedhead and a large T-shirt. Cain's shirt, Violet was guessing, judging by the way it hit at her upper thigh. Violet was only five five, but that T-shirt would leave her butt hanging out, and not in a sexy way.

Not that she had much opportunity to give it a try. Her and Keith's relationship hadn't been physical in ages, and even the couple of times they had slept together, almost out of obligation, she'd never thought to borrow one of his shirts.

Not that he'd offered.

"Hey, darlin'," Cain said, turning and giving the woman a slow, sleepy grin.

Violet blinked at the blatantly sexual charm. Where had he been hiding *that*?

The blonde wound her arms around his waist, resting her chin on his arm and gazing up at him, pointedly ignoring Violet, though she did glance at Coco. "Cute dog."

"Mmm," Cain said noncommittally before letting himself be drawn into a passionate, rather wet-sounding kiss.

Since they were too wrapped up in each other to pay attention or even remember she was there, Violet wrinkled her nose in distaste at the smacking noises.

The timer went off, and the woman unpeeled her mouth from Cain's, finally looking over at Violet. Her expression wasn't quite antagonistic, but the vibe was unmistakable: *this one's mine.*

Violet smiled pleasantly. *By all means.*

"Coffee?" Violet asked the two of them, turning to retrieve mugs from the counter.

"Yup," the woman said.

Yup, *please*, Violet mentally amended, the way she had been corrected in childhood until good manners had become as natural to her as breathing.

Violet went to the fridge. As expected, it was empty, save a six-pack of beer and a takeout container. She closed it again. "Black okay?"

The woman made a face. "Gross. Guess it'll have to be."

Violet's eyes caught Cain's just for a moment. *Really? This one?*

He merely gazed back at her, betraying nothing.

Violet pulled three mugs out of the cupboard, then realized that the small pot of coffee wasn't quite enough to fill up three mugs.

Because her ingrained hostess instincts wouldn't think of serving a measly half cup of coffee to guests in an effort to stretch it to three servings, she poured two full cups for Cain and his female companion, leaving none for herself.

She slid them both across the counter. Neither said thank you.

Violet bit back a sarcastic *you're welcome* and began rinsing out the grounds to make a second pot.

Cain startled Violet, coming up beside her, picking up her empty mug, and pouring half of his own coffee into it.

He unceremoniously set it on the counter in front of her.

Violet hid her surprise, not only that he'd shared his coffee, but that he'd even noticed she hadn't poured any for herself.

"Thank you," she told him.

He acted as though she hadn't spoken and leaned against the counter, mug in hand, one ankle crossed over the other, jeans still defiantly unbuttoned, with just a strip of . . .

Violet tore her eyes away and quickly resumed rinsing the glass carafe. She dried her hands, then picked up her mug, turning toward Cain's overnight guest. Since he seemed to have no inclination to introduce her to the other woman, she smiled and extended a hand. "Hello. I'm Violet."

"KC," she said, shaking Violet's hand with a blatantly curious once-over. "You Cain's rich cousin or something?"

"A *dear* family friend," Violet lied smoothly and without hesitation.

Cain snorted.

"Cool," KC said disinterestedly, rubbing under her eye and then looking at the black smudge on her finger. "Well, I gotta run. Gotta be at work in twenty."

"Where do you work?" Violet asked politely, hoping to lead Cain by example in the art of friendly small talk.

"Coffee shop in Midtown during the day. Bar in Yonkers at night. That's where I met Cain last night."

Violet smiled. "Well, that answers my next question of how long you've been seeing each other."

KC's eyes narrowed, as though trying to assess Violet's

level of snark. Then she shrugged, drained the rest of her coffee, and handed the mug to Violet. "Here. Already on thin ice with my shit manager 'cause I showed up stoned last week."

Violet accepted the mug and said nothing.

KC headed up the stairs, presumably to retrieve her clothes.

Violet set KC's mug in the sink. "More coffee?" she asked Cain, since he'd seemed to be drinking his in gulps.

She began making a second pot before he replied. *She needed more coffee to deal with him.* Actually, at this rate, she was gearing up for an afternoon glass of wine.

Out of the corner of her eye, she noticed Cain watching her carefully, as though taking note of the process, though his mask of indifference reappeared the second he caught her looking.

"So. Duchess. You care to explain the whole breaking-and-entering thing?"

"I didn't *break* anything," she clarified. "As for the entering, when you didn't answer, I figured you might be in the shower," she lied.

His eyebrows went up. "You thought I was in the shower, and you took that as your cue to come on in? Maybe this arrangement of ours will be more interesting than I thought."

He leaned toward her slightly, and the sheer maleness of him put her on edge.

"Would you please go put on some clothes?" she snapped.

Cain gave another of those insolent shrugs that seemed to be his favored form of communication. "You don't like it, you're welcome to leave the same way you came in. Go wander around a museum or something."

"I'm glad you mentioned museums," Violet said. "They're a bit of a New York institution, which means there will be *plenty* of those in your near future."

Cain didn't bother to disguise the grimace. "So, you were for real? You're really going to do this? Try to turn me into some sort of city douchebag just because the old lady told you to?"

"That *old lady* is your grandmother."

"The hell she is."

"But she said the blood tests came back—"

"Fuck the blood tests," he snapped. "You think that's what family is? Some shared blood? These people didn't give a single shit about me until they needed something."

"That may be true about Adam," Violet said, keeping her voice level. "But I know Edith almost as well as I know myself. There is no way she would have known about you and not gotten in touch. Now that she *does*, though, she's clearly doing her best to form a relationship with you—"

Cain interrupted rudely with a snort. "Form a relationship with me? She wants to turn me into a pretty boy puppet whose strings she controls."

"Oh, you poor thing," she said mockingly. "Let's not

forget that those strings are actually the reins of a *billion-dollar* company, not to mention a house to live in, free of charge—"

"Yeah, a real dream come true," he cut in caustically. "All I have to do is give up my home, my identity, my dignity . . ."

"Well, feel free to walk away," Violet said sweetly.

He wouldn't, of course. *Nobody* walked away from what Edith was trying to hand Cain Stone. The Rhodes fortune included access to a private jet, for God's sake.

"Fuck," he muttered, draining the rest of his coffee.

Violet sniffed. "The language is hardly necessary."

"*That's* unnecessary? Says the duchess in her old-lady pearls. How old are you, twenty-two going on ninety? Everything about you is unnecessary." He reached out and flicked an insolent finger over the necklace, and Violet stepped quickly back.

"Don't touch those," she said, her voice coming out in a protective snarl she barely recognized.

Cain froze, his eyes narrowing ever so slightly as though realizing his mockery had grated over a raw spot.

"Hey now," he said, his voice different than she'd heard it thus far. Lower, almost soothing. "I'm—"

If he was going to apologize—and that was a very big if—he was interrupted by the sound of KC clomping back down the stairs. Gone was the T-shirt. Instead she was wearing ankle boots, baggy black pants, and a tight tank top.

"Don't you have a jacket?" Violet asked before she could think better of it.

KC let out a mocking laugh. "I'll be fine, *Mom*."

Violet winced. She deserved that, though it stung on the heels of Cain's old-lady cracks.

KC blew Cain a kiss and headed toward the front door. He made no move to go after her.

Violet turned to him as the door closed.

Cain was looking at her. "A jacket? Really?"

"What?" she asked defensively. "It's cold outside."

"Jesus," he muttered. "Should I run after her and ask if she has a 401(k) and got the flu shot too?"

"He knows what a 401(k) is," Violet murmured under her breath, plunging the coffee. "That's a start."

Cain reached out, closing a hand over her wrist just as she was about to pour the coffee. "I'm not a hick," he snapped, close enough that she could feel his breath on her cheek.

"No? Prove it," she said smoothly, easing her hand away and refilling both of their cups. "Quit acting like a sulky child and button up your *fucking* pants already."

Five

*C*ain's only indication that he was surprised by her profanity was a single blink, but it was surprisingly gratify-
ing to have caught him off guard, if only for a moment.

For that matter, Violet had caught *herself* off guard.
Violet Victoria Townsend did not swear. Ever.

It felt illicit. It felt *great*.

Cain resumed his bored countenance, lifted a mocking
eyebrow. "Stepping out of our comfort zone, are we?"

"Is getting dressed out of *your* comfort zone, or do you
think you can manage?"

"You're certainly fixated on my state of dress, Duchess."

Violet wished she had a saucy rejoinder, but she'd used
up all her moxie on the F-word, and he knew it, because he
laughed softly as he moved away from her.

His laughter was replaced by a torrent of profanity that

put hers to shame as he stumbled a little. "Jesus, I almost stepped on your rat."

"She does tend to get underfoot," Violet admitted. "It's part of why I keep her in the purse."

Violet started to go to her dog, but Cain surprised her by scooping Coco up first, the tiny brown-and-black dog looking even tinier in his big hand as he held the Yorkie in front of his face and scowled at her.

Dog and man stared at each other for a long moment, as though taking stock of each other. Coco apparently liked what she saw, because she rewarded him with a lick on the nose.

Violet winced, braced for Cain's disgruntled response, but he surprised her by heading up the stairs, still carrying Coco.

"You're not going to kill her, are you?" Violet called after him.

He didn't respond.

When Cain came back down the stairs a few minutes later, he was wearing a faded gray T-shirt that was nearing threadbare, but at least his pants were buttoned. He was still holding Coco, the little dog resting comfortably on his forearm, cradled against his abdomen as though she belonged there.

When he came closer, she saw that his shirt wasn't plain, as she'd thought, but instead had a very faded pattern. She tilted her head as she recognized it. "Fleur-de-lis."

"What?" He sounded annoyed.

"That symbol on your shirt," she explained, pointing when he didn't reply. "It's the fleur-de-lis."

"I know what it is."

She smiled a little. "Did you know that's the same pattern I have on my powder room wallpaper?" Violet smiled. "You're dressed like the bathroom decorated by my grandmother."

Even beneath his beard, she could see his jaw grinding in irritation. "It's the logo for the New Orleans Saints."

She stared at him.

"Football team?"

Violet shrugged.

Cain just shook his head and went to the fridge. He shut it again, seeing it was empty, save the beer and leftovers.

She'd been counting on this and launched her initiative. "I was thinking we could go to breakfast. Discuss our game plan for this makeover mess we've found ourselves in."

He gave her a knowing look. "Changing our tack, are we? Pretending we're in this together?"

Aren't we, though?

"It's just breakfast," Violet pointed out with what she thought was admirable patience.

He lifted the dog to eye level, then looked back at her, shaking his head. "Toto and I say no."

"Coco."

"You basically carried her in here in a basket. We're going with Toto. Can you even take her into restaurants?"

"No," Violet admitted. "We'll have to drop her back at

my place. I shouldn't have brought her at all, but she looked so forlorn when I was leaving the house without her."

"That's one idea. Or"—he held up a finger—"you and Toto could *both* go to your house and stay there."

She pretended she didn't hear the suggestion. "What have you been eating since you've been here?"

"There's a bagel place around the corner. It works."

"Bagels aren't a bad way to warm up to New York, but you're never going to learn the city if you only stick within this block."

"So?"

She sighed. "If you're going to take over the business, you'll have to make peace with the city. It wouldn't kill you to at least *try* to learn your way around."

He crossed his arms. "It might."

Violet blew out her cheeks, reminding herself that he was *trying* to irritate her. It just came naturally. "If you're this recalcitrant about breakfast, you're going to hate shopping, aren't you?"

"Shopping?" He looked appalled.

"Yep, as I thought," she said. Then she tilted her head, trying yet another tack: bribery.

"The restaurant has bacon."

Both Coco's and Cain's ears seemed to perk up, though he quickly pasted his sarcastic mask back on. "Yeah, because that's all it takes to get a man to do what you want. The promise of bacon."

She merely checked her watch. Waited.

He hesitated. "How far is this place?"

"Walking distance. If you'll just go get dressed . . ."

He looked down. "I am dressed."

"You're *clothed*, yes. I mean dressed. For the day.

"To go out," she clarified when he continued to stare at her.

Nothing.

Suspicion mingled with alarm that things were more dire than she realized. To confirm the worst of her fears, Violet stepped around him and began heading up the stairs.

"What the hell are you doing?" he called after her, setting the dog on the floor and following her.

"Assessing your wardrobe options," she called.

The master bedroom was at the top of the hall, but a quick glance told Violet it hadn't been touched.

She paused in the doorway, tensing slightly when she felt Cain come up behind her, too close. Too large. Too male.

"I'm not sleeping in a dead man's bed," he said by way of quiet explanation as Coco danced around their ankles.

"Yeah, I don't blame you," she said softly. Downstairs, it had been easy to forget that the home once belonged to Adam Rhodes. Here, though, despite the fact that it had clearly been cleaned, all personal items removed, it seemed as though he could walk in at any time.

Violet instinctively stepped back, bumping into Cain's chest. For the second time that day, Cain steadied her, only this time his hand went to her waist, not her arms.

And lingered, thumb stroking in a caress.

She refused to react, knowing he was only trying to get a rise out of her. She wouldn't give him the satisfaction, even if her heart did seem to be beating a touch too fast.

"Are you done *handling* me?" she asked in a cool tone, her word choice a deliberate reference to their showdown in Edith's parlor a couple days earlier.

He laughed softly, his breath ruffling her hair. "Still thinking about that, are you, Duchess?"

Cain stepped back, clearly intending to go back down the stairs, but Violet continued down the hall, looking into the first door. Bathroom. The one he was using, judging by the toothbrush on the sink and the beat-up toiletry bag balanced on the narrow counter.

She went to the next room, noting the duffel bag on the chair and the rumpled bed, and forced herself not to linger too long thinking about that last one.

Violet opened the closet door, prepared to assess options for his nicer clothing items, but there was nothing but a few empty hangers.

She went to the duffel bag, hesitating only slightly before rifling through it.

"Yes, you're *definitely* the right person to teach me appropriate behavior," he drawled from the doorway, where he leaned, arms crossed as usual. "Breaking and entering. Stealing coffee. Rummaging through people's things . . ."

"I *made* you coffee," she said, pulling out a couple of wrinkled T-shirts and another pair of jeans, just as worn as the ones he was wearing. A pair of sweatpants. A lone blue sweater that had seen better days. Better *years*.

She turned to him, and it was on the tip of her tongue to ask where the rest of his clothes were, why he hadn't packed more, but the guarded look on his face stopped her.

"Apparently you weren't planning on staying in New York long," Violet said, gesturing toward the meager clothing options.

Cain shrugged and bent down to gently rub Coco's head with a knuckle. Violet ordered her heart not to melt. Or to think about the fact that Keith barely tolerated her dog's existence, much less pet the little Yorkie.

"I didn't think I'd be here more than a day or two," Cain said. "Certainly wasn't planning on the old lady trying to get me to stick around until Valentine's Day."

Valentine's Day. Even before Cain had shown up, Edith had planned to announce her board-approved successor at the famed Rhodes Heart Ball.

Violet had always looked forward to the black-tie affair, but this year, it felt more like a ticking time bomb.

She picked up the sweater and studied it. It was soft. Not

cashmere soft, but well-worn soft. "Why'd you come? To New York, I mean? You're clearly miserable about it."

Another shrug. "Curious. Enough to meet the old lady. Didn't plan on the whole family-legacy thing with her business."

"Or the incredible wealth that comes with it," Violet pointed out.

"Or that," he acknowledged, not the least bit embarrassed by the admission.

"It'll hurt her when you leave, you know," Violet blurted out. She hadn't meant to say it, but she cared too much about Edith not to worry.

He held her gaze a moment longer, then turned away, tossing a curt, "I'm hungry," over his shoulder.

Violet looked once more at the sweater, running a thumb over the threadbare fabric, then took it with her as she followed him down the stairs.

"Wear this," she said, pushing the sweater at his chest, then bending to scoop up Coco.

When she straightened, he was holding the sweater, but had made no move to put it on.

"What?" she snapped impatiently, unable to read his expression.

He shook his head and shoved his arms into the sleeves of the sweater, pulling it over his head. "Someday, Duchess, you're not going to get everything you want. I'd say I hope I'm around to see it, but with any luck, I'll be long gone."

He headed toward the front door, and Violet caught herself noting the way the sweater emphasized his broad shoulders, his jeans low on lean hips.

Violet had the sudden urge to tell him he was wrong.

She *didn't* always get what she wanted.

She didn't even know what that was.

Six

$\mathcal{V}$iolet hesitated in the doorway of the diner, her eyes scanning the window for the health-card rating that was in every New York restaurant. An A meant the place had achieved above a C rating . . .

Cain put a hand to her back, shoving her in the door before she could verify that the place wasn't crawling with rats.

A fifty-something waitress in a bright blue uniform paused, coffeepot in hand. "Two?"

She grabbed two menus from the hostess stand and headed toward a row of booths before waiting for confirmation.

Cain nudged Violet again, and she reluctantly followed, uncomfortably aware that she didn't look like she belonged. Most of the patrons were wearing jeans. A group of college-age kids were wearing pajamas. A couple of construction workers had their protective helmets on the table beside their ceramic coffee mugs.

Violet, in her heeled boots, Max Mara dress, and pearls, did not belong.

The waitress dropped the menus onto a table in a booth near the window, and Violet gingerly lowered onto the cracked vinyl seat.

"Coffee?" the waitress asked, flipping over the mugs.

"Yes, please," Violet said needlessly, not because she needed more coffee, but because the woman was already pouring.

"Know what you want or you need a bit?" the waitress asked.

Violet blinked. She hadn't even so much as touched the menu, which she sincerely hoped wasn't sticky, and—

"Give us a few," Cain said, smiling at the woman with a foreign friendliness that made him almost unrecognizable. Violet stared at him.

She did not like that grin.

It made him look . . . appealing.

The waitress smiled back at Cain, warm and a little flirty. "You got it, love."

The server resumed her coffee-filling rounds, and Violet tentatively used a fingernail to drag one of the menus to her. She caught Cain smirking and narrowed her eyes. "What?"

He leaned forward. "Admit it. Your snobbery is dying to point out everything wrong with this place."

"There's nothing wrong with it," she said quickly. "It's just . . . different."

"Then why'd you agree? Why not push for your fancy café?"

"Because you vetoed my place without stepping foot inside," she reminded him.

He studied her for a longer-than-comfortable moment. "And that's your thing? Agreeing to whatever someone else wants, no question?"

His tone was neither incredulous nor unkind, but the question scraped at something uncomfortable at the very back of her mind, so she lifted her menu and studied it.

"This menu is enormous," she said. "How can they possibly do everything well?"

"It's a diner, Duchess. Just pick something. Sorry it's not like your place, with its tiny tables, and miniature chairs, and the coffee costs four bucks. Let me guess, the menu has things like arugula and sunchokes and quinoa?"

Violet ignored the question, because her go-to order at Elliott's *did* just happen to involve arugula and quinoa.

He took a sip of the coffee, then winced slightly. "I'll give you a little credit, Duchess, your coffee is better than this place."

"It was actually Adam's coffee," Violet pointed out.

His expression turned stormy and sullen at the mention of his father, and Violet rubbed her forehead at the impending headache. Turning her attention to the menu, she saw that the omelet section alone seemed to have two dozen options, and there were nine different kinds of benedicts. How could one kitchen possibly do all of that well?

It couldn't, Violet decided. She set the menu aside, deciding to play it safe and simple.

The waitress came back their way and needlessly topped off both their coffees. "What can I get you?"

Cain picked up Violet's menu, stacked it on his, and handed both to the waitress, even though Violet hadn't seen him even open it. "I'll have pancakes, the Denver omelet, side of bacon. Sourdough toast. Actually . . . how are the biscuits?"

"For her"—the waitress pointed her pen at Violet—"they're fine. For you . . . stick with the toast."

"Why the different recommendation?" Violet asked curiously.

"Because I can tell from his accent he's from somewhere that makes biscuits better than we do," the waitress explained, before giving Violet an impatient look. "What are you having?"

"The fruit parfait, please," Violet said, earning an eye roll as the waitress walked away without writing it down.

"The fruit parfait?" Cain echoed, looked torn between amusement and disgust, leaning toward the latter.

She shrugged. "I like fruit. I like yogurt. It's not too heavy."

He opened his mouth, looking like he wanted to say

something, then shook his head and took a gulp of coffee as he turned to stare out the window.

Violet used the opportunity to study him.

He really was strikingly handsome, she had to admit, despite the fact that he was not at all her type. His eyelashes were thick and curved in a way that she couldn't achieve, even with the help of an eyelash curler. His dark hair was also thick and curly, pulled back in a messy knot at the nape of his neck, with just a few pieces escaping around his ears.

The truth was, he'd be downright pretty if not for the sharply defined jawline and dark facial hair that fell somewhere between stubble and scruff.

"Quit staring at me."

"Just trying to figure you out," she said, deliberately keeping her voice pleasant.

"I'm not your project." He looked back at her.

"Well, actually, you sort of are."

His jaw tensed, and he took another sip of coffee.

"Look," Violet said, folding her hands in her lap. "Let's be adults for a minute. You're going to have to decide. Either you don't want to go along with your grandmother's plan, and you let her and me know the arrangement is off. Or, you agree to it and get on board."

"I can be on board and not be happy about it."

"Sure," she nodded. "You could. If you were a sulky second grader, *absolutely* you could."

"Well, what the hell would *you* do, Duchess? Some long-lost relative barges into your life, turning everything upside down. I'm guessing it would ruffle even *your* passionless feathers."

Passionless. It was a strange sort of insult, and one that stung more than she'd have expected because it hit so close to home.

"I think I'd be grateful," she said, "to learn I even *had* family who wanted to know me."

He gave her a sharp look, and she realized she'd betrayed more than she meant to.

"Your grandmother," he said after a moment of silence. "She was a friend of Edith's?"

"Yes. She passed away when I was in college, but she raised me." Violet took a sip of the coffee, though it tasted even worse as it cooled.

"What happened to your parents?"

Violet's hand lifted instinctively to the pearls around her neck. "They died when I was eleven. They were in Costa Rica for a sightseeing tour. Their helicopter crashed."

Cain said nothing for a long moment. Then, "Sucks."

Violet smiled ruefully at the gruff assessment. "Yeah. But I'm lucky to have Edith. I was twenty-two when my grandmother died. Almost out of college, but honestly, I felt more child than adult. Edith was there for me on holidays, came to my graduation . . ."

"Must have been nice," he muttered.

Violet instinctively reached across the table, touching his hand. "She *really* didn't know about you, Cain. I know Edith. If she thought there was even the smallest chance she had a grandson out there, she'd have moved mountains to find you."

Cain shrugged as though it didn't matter, but she sensed it did. He didn't shake off her hand, just shifted back slightly to end the contact.

"I don't get you," she said quietly, returning her hand to her side of the table. "You seem to hate her, yet you're still here, going along with her plan, albeit reluctantly."

"You wouldn't get it."

"Try me."

Cain drummed his fingers once against the ceramic mug. "Most of my life has been shit. Some of it my own fault, some of it not."

His gaze dropped to the table. "As a kid, I spent a hell of a lot of time wishing things were different, that I'd been dealt a different hand. I guess when Edith's lawyer showed up on my doorstep, for a brief, idiotic moment, I was that kid again, thinking I'd finally been dealt a couple aces."

His expression was mostly twisted up in anger, but for the briefest of seconds, Violet thought she saw something else.

Longing.

Something she understood all too well. But though Violet typically excelled at making people feel comfortable, she didn't try to soothe with pretty words the way she would with someone else who was clearly hurting.

Instinct told her Cain Stone would throw it right back in her face.

Instead, she scratched her nose and then repeated back what he said when she'd told him about her parents. "Sucks."

Cain blinked, then let out a single bark of laughter. She'd surprised him again. She liked surprising him.

"What do you do? Back in Louisiana, for work?" she asked, wanting to keep him talking.

"Distribution company."

She waited for him to explain and bit back a sigh when he didn't, realizing that her makeover plan for the man would need to include the art of conversation.

"What's that entail?" she asked.

He looked surprised and a little annoyed by the question, as though he hadn't expected a follow-up. "Restaurant food distribution. The hospitality business is big in New Orleans. We transport oysters and shrimp to the fish markets, started supplying direct to some of the restaurants in the French Quarter. Other stuff too."

"Do you like it?"

"It pays the bills."

"That's not an answer," she said.

"It's the only one you're gonna get."

Violet wanted to protest but was interrupted by the arrival of their food. *Lots* of food, almost all of it placed in front of Cain.

She had to admit that by the time the waitress slid a plate of sourdough toast, shiny with butter, onto a bit of spare space near Cain's elbow, her fruit parfait looked rather unappetizing.

"All good?" the waitress asked.

Cain looked up. "Tabasco?"

"Right. Give me a sec."

Cain bit into a piece of bacon and noted Violet's expression. "Regrets?"

"Not one," she said primly, lifting her spoon, then cleaning it with her napkin when she noticed water spots.

Still chewing the bacon, Cain picked up the maple syrup, liberally doused the stack of pancakes, and pushed it toward her.

"Oh no, I'm fine," she said, gesturing with her spoon at the yogurt and meager sprinkling of not-quite-ripe berries.

Cain shook his head in annoyance and used his fork to hack off a bite of pancakes, then held it across the table to her, either not noticing or not caring when the syrup dripped onto the table.

"I'm fine," she repeated.

Cain lifted his eyebrows in challenge. Since avoiding a scene was second nature to her and he was standing his ground and people would likely start staring, she quickly accepted the bite of pancakes, mostly to end the awkwardness.

She began to chew, then stilled for a moment as she registered the sugary, decadent flavor. "Oh. Oh my."

Cain's eyes seemed to flash hot for a split second, only to be replaced quickly by his usual cutting smirk. "Maybe I can teach *you* something in all this, Duchess."

"Like what?" She dabbed at a bit of syrup on her lip.

He cut off a piece of his omelet, then caught her gaze. Held it. "Like the fact that life should be better than *fine*."

Seven

"Sorry, but this part is nonnegotiable. You need new clothes," Violet said, facing off with Cain as she gestured to the clothing store on the corner of Eighty-Fifth and Madison.

"So do what normal people do these days. Buy me a shirt online, and we'll call it good."

"No, we won't call it *good*. I like a good online shopping spree as well as the next person, but first we have to establish your signature style."

Whoops. Wrong choice of words for a man like Cain.

He stared at her a moment, then turned and unceremoniously walked away.

She hurried after him, caught his arm. "Okay, okay, I'm sorry. But look, we're already here. And you *did* tell Edith you'd try to fit in . . ."

He pulled his arm away from her angrily. "I can run a company just fine in what I'm wearing."

"Some companies, yes," Violet said calmly. "But not Rhodes. I get why you're resentful, I do. You want to be measured by your character, not your appearance. But in this world, the one Edith wants you to enter, impressions matter. *Clothes* matter."

Cain's eyes narrowed, then flicked to the store behind her, his wariness plain. "I don't want to come out of there looking like a damned Easter egg."

Violet smiled, hearing the statement for what it was: reluctant acquiescence. She gave his arm a reassuring pat. "Your coloring isn't suited toward pastels, so I think we're good."

"Oh, are we?" he said sarcastically. "Are we good?"

Violet held up her hands innocently. "It's your move, Cain. I'm not going to drag you in there like I'm your mother and it's time to do some back-to-school shopping."

He snorted. "Obviously you never met my mother."

Cain studied the storefront a moment longer, clearly having an internal war with himself. Violet wondered if those keen observational skills she'd noticed were working against him. He had to have taken note that that his worn jeans and faded T-shirt were out of place on Madison Avenue. And while he didn't strike her as the type of man to care about what others thought, or fitting in, he also didn't seem to be a man keen on failing.

"Do it for Edith?" Violet asked.

It was the wrong thing to say.

His expression shut down immediately, and his words were biting. "The grandmother I grew up wishing I had wasn't the kind to make her love conditional on how I dressed."

"Well, gosh, I'm sorry she's not dropping everything to serve you milk and cookies," Violet said, losing her patience with his determination to pick a fight on every front. "If you don't care about Edith, fine, but she's not the one you need to convince. It's the board members. And I can tell you right now, they're not going to vote you in if you look like you're on your way to go fishing."

He looked incredulous. "Fishing?"

She waved a hand. "Or whatever you like to do in your spare time."

His expression turned smoky. "Duchess, what I like to do in my spare time is a hell of a lot more pleasurable than *fishing.*"

Violet gave him a cool look, unperturbed by his efforts to push her buttons.

Well, okay, no, not *totally* unperturbed. She kept getting wafts of his clean, soapy smell, and she liked it more than she ought. She also noticed the way his sweater molded to his sculpted arms *way* more than she should.

His smirk told her he at least suspected her train of thoughts.

"Fine," Violet said with a cool smile as she started to turn away. "Keep roaming around the city dressed like my grandmother's wallpaper."

His fingers closed around her elbow, pulling her back around. His head dipped toward the store. "I'm not wearing pink."

"No pink," she agreed, crossing her heart with her pointer finger, then turning to enter the store before he changed his mind.

They both reached for the door handle, his hand closing over hers, and Violet froze at the contact, feeling absurdly preteen in her reaction to a simple touch of his hand.

To cover, she gave him a patronizing smile. "Opening doors for people. That's a solid start on the manners front."

He did have some. Not many, but there were hints. Sharing his coffee this morning. Holding doors. And he'd insisted on paying for breakfast and had generously tipped the waitress. More puzzling still, he'd made a point to tell the waitress thank you as they'd left the diner.

Violet tried to picture Keith even *entering* that diner, much less bothering to thank the waitress. Tried, and failed.

Which triggered a far more uncomfortable thought: Would *Violet* have thanked the waitress if Cain hadn't first? She always said please and thank you to waitstaff at restaurants, but to go out of her way as Cain had? She wasn't sure, and the realization was a bit jarring.

Violet stepped into the store, and they were immediately

greeted by a smiling salesman. Normally that sort of forward-ness annoyed her when she was just browsing, but she *wasn't* just browsing, and she needed all the help she could get.

She made a quick assessment of the man who introduced himself as Jacob, relieved by his low voice and calm de-meanor. Salespeople in New York could veer toward hyper, which would have lessened her chances of getting Cain to stay in the store for more than five minutes.

"Hello, I'm Violet," she said. "This is my friend Cain."

She thought she heard Cain snort at the word *friend*.

"What can I help you guys with today?" Jacob asked.

"Cain's new to the city," Violet said, deciding a direct ap-proach was best, with just a *touch* of white lie: "He's let me coax him into a New York makeover."

"Very good," Jacob said, nodding in a way that told Violet he heard everything she was saying, as well as every-thing she wasn't. "Come on back."

She started to follow, then turned and gave Cain a know-ing look. "After you."

Just in case he was thinking of bolting.

He shot her the briefest of scowls, then followed Jacob to a seating area near the dressing rooms.

Violet was relieved there were only a few customers in the store. It would make it all the easier for Cain if he didn't have an audience of curious shoppers.

"So, Cain, what brings you to the city?" Jacob asked over his shoulder.

Violet nearly laughed. What was normally an innocuous question had a whopper of an answer.

Well, let's see. In order to inherit billions, he has to convince the biggest snobs in all of Manhattan that he's not straight out of the bayou, which . . . he sort of is.

"Business," Cain said curtly.

Violet rubbed her fingers between her eyebrows and mentally noted they had some serious work to do on his small talk skills.

Jacob nodded amiably and gestured toward a couple of straight-backed chairs. Violet sat. Cain did not.

"What are we looking for today?" Jacob asked.

"A little of everything," Violet said before Cain could respond with something profane. "An overcoat, definitely. I loved the look of that gray wool one in the window. Slacks and dress shirts. Maybe a couple more casual options too," she said quickly, catching Cain's thunderous expression.

"Absolutely. Cain, you mind if I take some measurements?" Jacob asked, pulling out a measuring tape.

Cain did mind. It was obvious from his frown, but he stood in front of a full-length mirror and tolerated Jacob measuring his inseams, the width of his shoulders.

Broad, Violet noted. *Very broad.*

"If you'll hang tight for just a minute, I'll be right back with some options to get us started," Jacob said, glancing down at his notebook and wandering off.

Cain dropped into the seat beside her. She looked at him. "How are we doing?"

He frowned. "Don't give me that *we* shit. You're not the one on display."

"True. Instead, I get to live out my life's dream of babysitting a sulky man-child."

"And yet you agreed to the old lady's plan," he said, sitting back in the chair. "Makes me wonder just how boring your life must be."

"My life isn't boring," she retorted automatically.

"Yeah? What would you normally be doing right now, if not dressing me up like a Barbie doll?"

"Trust me, you're hardly a Barbie doll. More angry GI Joe," she said, dodging the question so she didn't have to reply that she'd likely be running errands for Edith, though most definitely of an easier variety than the one she was tasked with currently.

Jacob rejoined them with an enormous stack of clothes. He directed Cain to a dressing room as he patiently explained what shirt went with which pants, what was brunch casual, which was cocktail casual . . .

"Don't forget, we're expecting a fashion show out here," Violet called out sweetly as Cain pulled the heavy black curtains to the dressing room closed. His hand shot back through the opening, middle finger extended.

Violet was so startled she laughed.

As Cain changed, Violet mentally readied her platitudes for when the curtain reopened. She was good at saying the right thing. All of Edith's friends believed her when she assured them they had no wrinkles. She was the first one her friends called when needing promises that *of course* they could get their prebaby body back. She'd even convinced Keith that his hairline wasn't already receding, and that was quite a feat, because it totally was.

In other words, Violet was armed and ready with pretty flatteries to reassure Cain that yes, he could pull off dress slacks and cashmere, even if he looked ridiculous.

As it turned out, she didn't need platitudes. Or flattery. Or lies. And he did not look ridiculous.

When he stepped out into the main area, Violet could barely keep her jaw from dropping.

Cain Stone didn't just *pull off* the dark gray slacks and pale blue sweater. He *owned* them. Everything fit him to perfection, as though they were tailor-made instead of off the rack.

"Excellent," Jacob murmured, studying Cain in a polite, but assessing way. "You know, I don't even know if we need the pants altered. They fit you just right."

Yeah they did. Violet was feeling a bit . . . warm

"How's everything feel?" Jacob asked Cain.

Cain shrugged. "Like clothes."

Jacob glanced at Violet, looking for more help. "Thoughts?"

Violet swallowed, her mouth strangely dry. "Nice."

Cain lifted his eyebrows, and there was a smokiness to

his gaze when his brown eyes found hers. Her voice had been . . . breathy.

"Let's try the light gray sweater with the same pants," Jacob said, either oblivious to, or ignoring, the sparks between Cain and Violet. "I think you'll like the monochromatic look."

Violet wasn't sure if Jacob was talking to Cain or to her, but as Cain tried on the next set of clothes, she decided *she* definitely liked the monochromatic look for Cain.

Just as she liked the white button-down.

The burgundy sweater.

The gray slacks, the navy chinos.

Even an olive-green cardigan, which should have been dowdy but instead seemed to bring out flecks of gold in his eyes that she hadn't noticed before.

Jacob seemed to sense the precise moment when Cain was ready to wave the white flag, because he handed over a stack of T-shirts, and she could tell by the way Cain's shoulders were just slightly less hunched in defense when he came out of the dressing room that the T-shirts were his favorite of everything he'd tried.

She watched in amusement as Cain absently checked the price tag, then blinked a little too rapidly. *Welcome to quality, my friend.*

He gave Violet an angry, incredulous look, which Jacob was astute enough to catch. The store employee held up a finger. "You know, I've *just* thought of a coat we have in the front that I want you to take a look at. Give me one minute."

Violet smiled distractedly in thanks as he walked away, knowing that he was actually giving *them* a minute, and grateful for it.

She stood and walked over to Cain, giving him a reassuring smile. "You look great."

"It's a two-hundred-dollar shirt. A cadaver would look great in it." He reached around to his back, trying to find the tag of the pants.

Violet reached out and grabbed his hand, knowing that while the price tag was modest by New York shopping standards, all of the items cost a good deal more than the jeans he'd walked in with.

Cain went still, giving her a sharp look, before deliberately dropping his gaze to their joined hands.

She released him quickly and stepped back. She ran a hand over her skirt under the guise of smoothing it, but really it was to stop the strange tingling in her hand from where they'd made contact.

"I don't mean to be crass," she said quietly so as not to be overheard. "But Edith mentioned she'd requested some credit cards with your name on them—"

"Yeah. I can pay for this shit, I just don't know why I *would*."

"Because you look good in them," she insisted.

"By your standards. You and your yuppy friends."

Violet inhaled for patience. "My yuppy friends' standards are exactly the ones you'll need to meet—*exceed*—if you want to take over the family business. And let's just rip off this Band-Aid right now: if these prices are freaking you out, we're going to sedate you before we go suit shopping."

"I have a suit."

Suit. Singular. Something told her it was probably black, ill-fitting, and reserved for funerals.

"Great! Maybe someone back home can ship it to you?" she chirped, deliberately agreeable to deprive him of the opportunity to pick a fight.

His jaw twitched. "How much are the suits you have in mind?"

She made a demurring noise. "Let's work up to that number, shall we?"

He made a growling noise but didn't push the issue. "Are we done here?"

"You've only tried on a handful of options. Out of"—she pulled aside the curtain to the dressing room to see the remaining items—"one million."

"I don't need—"

Jacob approached with two wool coats from the window display over his arm, and Violet crossed over to him immediately, running a hand over the high-quality wool. "*Yes*. These. They're even better up close."

Violet turned back to Cain, who'd succeeded in fishing

out the price tag on his pants. She held up the dark gray overcoat. "Perfect."

He opened his mouth, and she shoved the coat at his chest firmly to shut him up. "Put this on."

Before Cain could protest, she turned back to Jacob. "That T-shirt he's got on. Does it come in other colors?"

"Absolutely. Black, white, gray, maroon, a deep purple, hunter green—"

"We'll take one in every color in his size. How about the pants? Are there more color options?"

"Just a few; there's the charcoal he has on now, a lighter gray, and a black."

"Perfect, all three of those." She glanced over her shoulder. "Cain, of the sweaters, did you like the V-neck or the crew neck?"

"I don't give a sh—"

She stepped toward him, reaching up and adjusting the collar of the coat he'd put on, mostly to silence him. "Perfect. This is just perfect."

"Does this come in orange too?" Cain asked Jacob sarcastically. "Or eight other shades of gray?"

"This one will do," Violet said, patting Cain's chest just a little more firmly than was affectionate. "Now about the sweaters, I think V-neck."

Jacob was nodding. "So he can layer over the T-shirts for a pop of color."

"A pop of—do I even need to be here?" Cain asked incredulously.

"Yes, because we need to see how the more casual chinos fit you."

"The what?"

She went into the dressing room, digging through the pile until she found the pants in navy. "These. Try with the off-white sweater."

"Then we're done."

It wasn't a question, and from the stubborn set of his jaw, Violet knew this was the most cooperation she was going to get from day one of his "transformation."

"All right," she relented.

"Good. Then I need a drink."

"It's barely noon."

He ignored this point and fixed her with a dark glare. "Do you know how much this is going to cost?"

"Um—"

Cain named an exact figure, and Violet did a double take. "You added that up in your head?"

"A drink," he said, lifting a finger in warning and ignoring the question. "You're buying."

He shut the curtain to the dressing room with a snap, and Violet turned to Jacob. "We'll be wrapping up after this. But can I get your card? I'd like to bring him back to look at your blazers."

She heard Cain muttering curses behind the curtain.

"Some other day," she whispered to Jacob. He nodded knowingly.

Eight

"*L*emongrass rooibos okay?" Violet asked, carrying her great-grandmother's tea set into her living room and setting it on the glass coffee table.

Ashley Shores turned away from the record player in the corner, Ella Fitzgerald album in hand. "Perfect. We haven't had that yet—have we??"

"Tea Thyme had it on sale the other day," Violet said, referring to the local loose leaf tea shop around the corner from her apartment. "I have about a dozen other varieties to use up, but I couldn't resist."

"Just like I can never resist Ella," Ashley said with a happy sigh as Ella's warm, rich version of "Misty" filled the room.

Kicking off her pristine white tennis shoes, Ashley tucked her legs beneath her, curling up in her usual spot in the corner of the settee. Coco had been playing with her champagne bottle squeaker toy on the carpet, but she jumped up beside her Auntie Ashley and hunkered down in her familiar Sunday afternoon routine. Violet sat in *her* usual chair and began the familiar process of pouring tea, a splash of milk and one spoonful of sugar for herself, a half spoonful of sugar and no milk for Ashley.

Ashley had been one of Violet's closest friends growing up, her partner in crime at slumber parties, the one who'd tried valiantly to coax Violet's straight hair into "power curls" before a debate club tournament, the one she'd called when Brendan Glaxter had broken her heart in sixth grade, and the one who'd brought over Reese's Pieces when Matt Casey had dumped Violet for Rosemary Nowak their junior year.

They'd drifted a bit in college; Violet had stayed on the East Coast, attending Brown, while Ashley went to the California Institute of Technology. But both had returned to the city after graduation and picked up right where they'd left off, though they'd traded their weekly Friday night sleepovers for Sunday afternoon tea.

It was one of Violet's favorite parts of the week. After she'd escorted Edith to church, after the social butterfly Ashley had attended one of her many brunch invitations, the two friends always found themselves here, in Violet's quietly old-fashioned living room, listening to old music and sipping tea from the rose-patterned china set that had belonged to Violet's *great*-grandmother.

"So," Ashley said, blowing on her tea with pursed lips before setting the cup and saucer aside and pulling her shoulder-length, wavy blond hair into a knot at the nape of her neck. "The prodigal grandson. Tell me *everything*."

Violet had texted Ashley the gist of her predicament earlier in the week, but she hadn't yet had a chance to bring Ashley, or any of her friends, up to speed on the full magnitude of the undertaking that was Cain Stone.

She sighed and blew softly on her own tea. "I don't even know where to begin."

"I do," Ashley said matter-of-factly. "He's hot."

Violet looked up. "How do you know?"

"Um, the Internet? I looked him up the second you told me about him. He's not particularly active on social media, but he has an account with a picture." She fanned herself, then looked worried. "Tell me he didn't just post a glamour shot and is actually a troll in real life."

"No, he's attractive," Violet admitted. "In a rugged, bad boy sort of way. If you're into that."

"Sweetie, *everyone's* into that," Ashley said. "The bad boy thing is irresistible. It's a fact."

"Not irresistible to *me*," Violet said, though the past couple days had her questioning her stance on that.

"True," her friend admitted. "Keith is as far from bad boy as they come. I bet his onesies were made out of argyle cashmere. Not that he isn't handsome!" she rushed to assure Violet.

Violet smiled at the too-enthusiastic exclamation. Ashley would never speak an *overtly* bad word against Keith, but she'd never done a good job of disguising the fact that she didn't particularly like him. The two were mostly polite to each other if forced to be in the same room, but they'd never clicked.

Keith was less subtle in his dislike. He'd been known to drop the word *flighty* when Ashley's name came up, no matter how staunchly Violet reminded him that for all Ashley's bubbly mannerisms, she was also a clinical research assistant in genetics.

"So, here's my issue with this whole thing," Ashley said, picking up her teacup and taking a careful sip to test the temperature. "As much as I understand Edith's desire for a legacy, doesn't this *My Fair Lady* thing feel sort of . . . messed up?"

"I don't think she wants Cain to change who he is as a person," Violet said, instinctively defending Edith. She snagged a butter cookie off the china plate and took a bite. "She just wants to tweak the packaging."

"Hmm. How does Cain feel about that?"

Violet grunted indelicately as she popped the rest of the cookie into her mouth. "About what you'd expect from someone whose idea of formalwear is denim without holes in the knees."

"Ah. So an uphill battle."

"You have no idea." Violet dusted the crumbs off her

fingers. "Clothes shopping wasn't *as* bad as I expected. But then on Friday I took him to the Frick Collection, trying to teach him that in Edith's world, the appreciation of art is nearly as respected as the art itself."

"If not more so," Ashley said with a grin.

"Right! You get it. Cain, not so much. He refused to even *practice* that appreciative but noncommittal murmur we've all been taught to perfect when asked our opinion of a sculpture that looks just like every other sculpture in the room."

Ashley demonstrated the exact noise, a low, almost throaty sound of approval and enthusiasm, as though too moved and contemplative to actually speak to the nuances of the art piece.

Violet laughed. "If only *you* were my pupil."

To say that Cain had been a poor student at the museum would have been an understatement. She supposed she should be happy he'd agreed to meet her at all, but he'd lasted all of thirty minutes before declaring he had better things to do with his Friday afternoon than look at "old crap."

She hadn't bothered texting him yesterday. She figured they could both use a break before more "training" tomorrow.

"It's early days yet," Ashley reassured her. "If anyone can turn him into the perfect Manhattan robot, it's you."

Violet looked quickly down at her tea to hide her discomfort at the assessment.

"Oh damn," Ashley said, setting her saucer on the table with a clatter, startling Coco in the process. "I did not mean that like it sounded. It was intended as a compliment, I swear," Ashley said, looking distraught.

"I know." Violet reassured her with a smile. Ashley didn't seem to notice that the smile was forced. Nobody ever noticed, not her best friend, not Keith, not even Edith. "You're not wrong. I mean, look at my home."

"It's beautiful," Ashley said, looking around at the ornate decor. "You know I love it here. It's like stepping back in time."

Her friend meant *that* as a compliment too, Violet knew, but it rubbed at a nerve, newly exposed. She'd never given much thought to the style of her home before; it was simply where she'd lived ever since her parents had died. And even before then, she'd spent a fair amount of time there visiting her grandmother. The three-bedroom unit was beautiful in a classic kind of way. The type of building with the original elevator and marble floors that had been installed a century earlier, the facade updated only as much as safety necessitated.

As an honor to the building and her grandmother, Violet had left the apartment alone, save for upgrading appliances and getting air-conditioning installed to better endure the stifling summer months in the city. But the furniture, the wallpaper, the artwork, even the dishes had stayed the same.

Most of the time, Violet loved living in an homage to another time, another generation. But increasingly lately she felt like she was the one living in a museum, and the people around her were the ones making noncommittal sounds of approval toward her, like she was aesthetically lovely but not all that interesting in her own right.

The apartment no longer felt old-fashioned; she just saw old. It didn't feel so much elegant and timeless, as . . . *stuck.* And the more she dwelled on it, the more she knew the apartment was merely a representation of Violet herself.

Tired. Dated. Boring . . .

She shoved the thoughts aside, the way she always did.

"I'm already sort of regretting agreeing to Edith's plan," Violet admitted to her best friend. "I pride myself in being able to do anything Edith asks of me without question, but I've never met anyone like him."

"How so?"

"He's . . ." Violet blew on her tea, trying to find the words to describe Cain. "Angry. That was my first thought when I met him: he's got a lot of anger coming off him. At Adam, and Edith, at the whole situation."

"Can you blame him? He's got to feel a little bit robbed, looking at what his childhood could have been if his biological father hadn't been such an ass."

"True. But it's being handed to him *now*," Violet said.

"With some pretty annoying caveats," Ashley added gently. "It would be a tough pill for anyone to swallow."

"I suppose," Violet admitted. "Still doesn't explain why the guy can barely be bothered to put on pants."

Ashley nearly snorted her tea. "I'm sorry, what?"

"Long story," Violet said, waving her hand.

"And one I'd like to hear in extreme detail," Ashley said with a cheeky grin.

After Violet brought her friend up to speed on her first morning at Cain's house, as well as describing his overnight guest, she lifted her hands in helpless frustration. "You see? The man has no idea how to behave, no clue how to fit in, and I don't even think he wants to."

"Hmm." Ashley pressed her lips together and got that distant expression that Violet recognized as her science-minded analytical face. "Maybe that's part of the problem," she said after a long moment.

"The problem is that he's prone to sullen silences and wore a faded bomber jacket to the Frick on Friday instead of the wool peacoat I specifically told him to wear."

"Well, yeah, there's that," Ashley agreed. "But to be fair, do *you* like going to the Frick?"

"Not particularly," Violet admitted after a moment.

"What about shopping? Because as I recall, we're both known to get more excited about free shipping and returns than window-shopping these days. And," Ashley continued, "you're wearing makeup and your pearls, but—" She waved a finger at Violet's bottom half. "Yoga pants."

Violet narrowed her eyes good-naturedly. "Do I even want to know where you're going with this?"

"What's that phrase your grandma used to love? Something about bugs and honey?"

"You can catch more flies with honey than with vinegar," Violet said without hesitation. Her grandma *had* loved that phrase.

"Exactly. There you go," Ashley said with a confident nod, as though everything was clear now.

"I don't follow. You think I've been serving up vinegar?" Violet asked, trying not to be offended.

"Not exactly. I mean, on the *surface*, your plan makes sense. The guy is going to have to learn to endure wearing a tie and tolerate museums, you're right on about that. But come on, Vi. That's not all New York is—it's not all we are. It's not why we love it, it's not why we live here. Right?"

"I guess so," Violet said slowly. "But I don't see where you're going with this."

"I just think maybe he'd find the shopping and ties and museums in his future a bit more palatable if you cushioned the boring stuff with parts of New York he'll actually *like*."

"So far, the only things he's confessed to liking are bagels and sex."

"Well, who doesn't?" Ashley grinned.

"I'm all for catching the fly, but I am *not* giving Cain Stone that kind of honey," Violet said, even as the thought of Cain and sex in the same sentence made her a little bit warm and irritable.

Ashley's answering grin was pure mischief. "Not at *all* what I was suggesting, but interesting that you thought it was."

Nine

*N*ow where are we going?" Cain asked dubiously, following Violet through the stone entrance. "I swear to God, woman, if you're dragging me to another hushed museum . . ."

"No museum today," she said pleasantly as she lifted Coco out of her purse, clipped on her leash, and set the little dog on the dirt path. "Mr. Stone: welcome to Central Park."

Cain narrowed his eyes suspiciously at her, then turned his attention toward their surroundings.

"Huh," he said, looking around at the famous urban oasis as they walked farther into the park. Coco darted quickly to her left, barking furiously at movement in the bushes.

Cain looked amused. "Um, Duchess, hate to be the one to tell you this, but Toto is chasing after a rat bigger than she is."

"You *love* being the one to tell me that," Violet said. "But yeah, she does that. You'll get used to it."

He glanced down, surprised. "Are *you* used to it?"

"Of course. I mean, it's not as though I'd tolerate rats running through my house or in a restaurant. Here?" She shrugged. "It's their home too. That's the beauty of Central Park."

"If you say so."

"You don't have rats in New Orleans?"

"We do." He lifted his shoulders. "I just don't get romantic about it. Not the cockroaches either."

"Don't worry, we have those too," Violet said. "You should feel right at home."

"Don't bet on it."

Violet made no reply to that. She was learning that when Cain wanted to be surly, which was pretty much always, it was best to let him have at it.

They walked in silence for a few moments, headed in no direction in particular, which was sort of the point of Central Park; none of the paths went in a straight line.

"What do people do here?" Cain asked, though he sounded more curious than derisive, and she didn't think it was her imagination that he seemed slightly more relaxed here than he did on the bustling sidewalks.

"Just what you see," she said, gesturing around. "They go for a run. Push strollers. Walk dogs. Skateboard. Sit. Read.

It's busier in the summer, especially on weekends. There's live music, Shakespeare plays, picnics."

Violet tilted her head back a little to take in the birds sitting on bare tree branches, the white sky that looked like it would hold true to the forecast of snow later in the evening. "It's really beautiful in spring and summer. Green, lush, warm. But this is actually my favorite time of year. There's nothing quite like winter in Central Park."

Cain looked over at her, and though he said nothing, he seemed to invite her to continue.

Violet inhaled the cool air deeply. "It's less crowded, the ponds freeze over, and everything just seems so beautifully *still*. Like you've walked into this silent, peaceful moment in time. It's even better when it snows. Out on the streets, everything gets slushy and dirty fast, but here it stays a winter wonderland just a bit longer."

He made an unimpressed sound.

"You don't like snow?" Violet asked.

"I've barely seen snow," he said. "We're more of a hurricane kind of town, and those rarely go well for us."

"Ah. Right. Well, you might get a chance later today. Just a dusting. A good introductory snow."

They paused so Coco could do her business, and after Violet had picked up and disposed of the evidence, Cain shifted so he stood in front of her.

"Give it to me straight, Duchess. What are we doing

here? What are you buttering me up for? Walking lessons? Dialect classes? Some fussy auction?"

"Nothing like that," she said truthfully. "I just thought you might like a day to be in the city without having an agenda."

He narrowed his eyes and, apparently satisfied with what he saw in her expression, rolled his shoulders a little, as though trying to relax. "I'm hungry."

She laughed. "I thought you just ate lunch before we met up."

"I did."

"All right," she said, sucking in her cheeks as she considered their options. "There aren't a lot of restaurants in the park. And most close down in the winter, but we could try—"

"How about that?" Cain interrupted, pointing.

She turned and saw one of the many stands throughout the park that offered hot dogs, soda, and not much else.

"Sure," she said skeptically, and needlessly, since he was already descending upon it.

Violet followed, overhearing just as he ordered a hot dog, instructing the vendor to not be stingy with the mustard. Cain glanced over. "Want anything?"

Violet shook her head. Cain looked down at her feet. "Coco? Want a wiener?"

"No," Violet said with a firm laugh. "Not unless you're picking up the inevitable mess that will follow."

The corner of his mouth tilted up as he plucked a Coke out of the ice bin. "One of these too."

The bored-looking vendor nodded and reached for the twenty Cain held out.

"Actually," Violet said before she even realized she meant to speak. "I'll have a pretzel. Please. I'll pay you back," she added to Cain.

"Don't worry about it," he said, accepting the hot dog as well as the enormous soft pretzel wrapped partially in a sheet of parchment paper.

He handed the pretzel to Violet, and she took it almost reluctantly, not entirely sure what had prompted the spontaneous request. She hadn't had a soft pretzel in . . . she couldn't even remember.

They stepped away from the cart, and Cain nodded in the direction of a crowd and music. "What's that?"

"Ice-skating rink. You interested?"

"In watching? Sure."

A few moments later they nestled up to the railing and watched the skaters, some of them expertly circling, others awkwardly clambering along the outside edge. Level of skill seemed to have no bearing on the skaters' happiness level; everyone was smiling.

Cain ate half the hot dog in one bite, chewing it slowly, methodically as he took in the scene. "Bite?" he asked, holding out the hot dog to her. Violet shook her head, though poor Coco wagged her tail hopefully.

Violet broke off a chunk of the pretzel and took a bite, studying the uneaten bit as she chewed. She doubted it would win any pretzel awards. It was a little tough. The salt had been distributed in uneven patches. The tips where the ends crossed over the center loops were a bit too browned.

But it tasted amazing.

"Good?" Cain asked, and she realized his attention had shifted from the skaters to her.

"*So* good," she said, eating with more enthusiasm now.

He finished off the last of his hot dog in a bite, and after tossing his wrapper into the nearby trash, broke off a piece of her pretzel without asking and ate that too. Only the tiniest part of her brain considered pointing out the rudeness of his action, because it didn't *feel* rude. It felt oddly companionable, and when he bent down to give a tiny piece of the pretzel to Coco, something unfamiliar fluttered in her chest.

She took a couple of more bites, more because it felt right in the moment than because she was actually hungry, then handed the rest to him, which he polished off quickly.

In silent agreement they began walking again, wandering among the dirt paths, zigzagging from east to west, meandering farther uptown and then cutting back south again.

"I see why you like it here."

She carefully hid her smile of triumph that her mission was thus far successful: finding a little corner of the city he didn't loathe.

"You walk here every day?" he asked.

"No, not every day. And not usually this far. But I try to get here a few times a week. Coco loves it, and it's a refreshing break from the car horns and subway rumbles."

"I bet Toto would love it more if she didn't have to wear that ugly sweater," he said, jerking his head at the dog, who was zipping back and forth in front of them, inspecting every leaf, every mound of dirt.

"She likes her sweater!"

"No, Duchess. She doesn't." He took a deep breath. "You and Toto always come to the park alone?"

There was a slight emphasis on the last word.

"Usually. Sometimes I can coax Edith into getting a bit of fresh air."

"What about romantic strolls with some stuffy suit?"

She looked over sharply.

"Ah," he said with a laugh. "So there *is* a stuffy suit in the picture."

"Keith is not stuffy."

"And yet, *Keith* came to mind when I said the words *stuffy suit*. What's the story there? I don't see a ring."

"I'm wearing gloves," she pointed out.

"You weren't the first day we met, and I didn't see one then either."

"You looked?" she asked.

He lifted an eyebrow. "You care?"

She sniffed and focused on Coco darting around in her little red-and-white-striped sweater, which she did *too* like. "We're not engaged," she said. "Just . . . sort of dating."

"'Sort of dating,'" Cain repeated mockingly. "Meaning, he's screwing you when he feels like it but won't commit?"

"Why do you always have to be like that?" she snapped. "Crude and rude and . . . *awful.*"

"Because it's the fastest way to cut through your fake-ass bullshit," he said impatiently. "Because it's easier to read you when you look like *this.*"

He nodded downward, as though to indicate her current facial expression.

"And what," she asked, coming to a stop and glaring at him, "do I look like?"

"Honestly?" he said, stepping toward her.

She nodded, though a bit warily.

Cain stepped even closer. "You look like a woman who hasn't been properly fu—"

Without thinking, Violet's hand flew up to his face, resting the tips of her fingers over his mouth. "Do not finish that sentence. I know it's your favorite word, but you don't get to say it to me. Especially not in that context."

Neither of them moved, anger swirling around and between them as they faced off.

His lips parted, and she felt a puff of warm air against her fingertips that caused an immediate answering pull low in her stomach.

Dangerous.

She snatched her hand back as though he'd burned her.

"So the royal duchess has a pulse after all," he said gruffly. More statement than apology.

She swallowed. "Keith and I have been together for years. I won't have what he and I share belittled by someone I've known less than a week."

Coco seemed to sense her owner's agitation and trotted back to them, anxiously skittering around their ankles as they argued.

Cain continued to gaze at Violet with mocking eyes. "I think you're more pissed at yourself than me, because you don't know the answer to a simple question."

"Was there a question? All I heard was you being a jerk."

"Sure there was a question." Cain moved closer, his thumb pressing at the very center of her chin, lifting her face upward. "Are you his girl? Or are you not?"

Violet let out a breathless laugh. "Am I his *girl*? What is this, 1912?"

"That's not an answer." He studied her closely. "Then again, maybe it is."

"Make whatever assumptions you like. I'm nobody's girl. Woman," she added, hating how flustered she felt by the question.

"Damn shame, Duchess," he said, stepping back and looking bored. "I've gotta say, the more I see of your life, the worse it looks."

"You're insufferable," Violet muttered, pivoting away from him to end their standoff. Only Coco, for all her tiny size, had managed to tangle her leash around Violet's ankles, and she stumbled slightly.

Cain's hands came out to steady her, just as Coco did another agitated lap, looping the leash around his ankles as well, then ran off after a bird, the shortened tether bringing the dog up short and pulling the leash taut around their legs.

Violet tried to step out of the loop, as did Cain, which only tangled them further.

"Stop," he commanded, and Violet froze, both from the firm tone in his voice and the feel of his palm pressing against her back. Even through her coat and sweater, she swore she could feel the heat of his hand and had the inexplicable urge to press closer.

Her heart beating harder than it should, she glanced up, and he stilled as their eyes locked, him looking as puzzled as Violet by the strange pull between them that had nothing to do with the leash.

He shook his head slightly and pulled her closer to him. For a moment Violet thought it was an embrace, that he might kiss her there in the middle of Central Park.

Almost as quickly, she realized he'd only pulled her closer to loosen the slack of the leash so he could step out, one foot, then the other. He released her and knelt down, scooping up Coco and unclipping her leash.

Violet bent and untangled her leather boots from the red leash as Cain gently but firmly placed Coco back in her purse.

"She wants to walk," Violet protested, only to frown when Coco made two full turns within the bag, the way she did when preparing to nap, then happily curled into a tiny ball.

Cain's smile was smug.

"Congratulations," she sweetly. "If only you read women half as well as you read female dogs."

"I read you better than you know, Duchess."

"I hate that nickname," she snapped.

"Well, if we all got everything we wanted, I wouldn't be here," he shot back.

"Here right now in the park, or the situation at large?"

His jaw ticked, and he looked away. "I don't hate the park."

Violet hid her smile. As far as progress went, it was next to nothing, but it was still something.

"So what's next?" Cain asked warily. "A lecture on the evils of clip-on bow ties? Suffering through the theater?"

"It's Monday," Violet said.

"And?"

"Broadway's dark on Mondays."

"Hold on a sec, give me a chance to write that down," he deadpanned.

She looked to the sky. "You forgot to tell me what to do if I don't *want* to catch the fly."

"What are you going on about?"

"Chatting with my grandmother about honey and vinegar," she said. "Okay, so you're not into theater. Noted. Anything you do like? Besides sex and sulking?"

His very white teeth flashed briefly, as though his grin caught him by surprise, and he had to recover to wipe it away. "I have some hobbies."

"Edge of my seat here," she said as they walked again.

Cain said nothing, and she glanced over, a little surprised to see he seemed almost embarrassed.

"Needlepoint?" she prodded.

He rolled his eyes. "I read. And I like jazz."

Her head whipped around, pulse thrumming. "Jazz?"

She *loved* jazz.

Cain lifted a shoulder. "Mock all you want. Doesn't matter anyway. Nobody does it like New Orleans."

"Oh, I wasn't mocking," Violet said earnestly. "But you should start preparing now."

"For?"

She smiled. "To eat your words."

"No! You have to fold it."

"*Fold it?*" Cain asked, the pizza paused halfway to his face as he shot her an incredulous look. He glanced down at the paper plate, then shrugged. He picked up the pointy part of his pepperoni slice and began folding it back to the crust.

"No," Violet said with a laugh. "The other way."

She reached out and curled both ends of the crust toward each other. "There. Like that."

Violet did the same with her own cheese slice, and together they took a bite at the same time.

She closed her eyes in pleasure as the salty, chewy, tangy flavors rolled over her tongue. Even better than the pretzel.

When she opened her eyes, she found Cain watching her, though his gaze cut away the second it met hers, and he took another large bite.

"So? Verdict on your first New York slice?" she asked.

"Good," Cain admitted. "Not as good as the jazz, but it hits the spot."

"I told you," she said smugly, picking a string of cheese off her plate and eating it. "The jazz clubs here are *amazing*."

"As promised," he said. Cain looked down at his pizza. Frowned. "Thanks for staying for the double set."

"Are you kidding?" she asked as they began making their way downtown, pizza still in hand. "I loved it. I can barely find anyone to go to shows with me, and definitely no one to stay for two."

He gave her a surprised look. "You really are a jazz fan."

"Did you think I was lying?"

"Yup."

"Does it ever occur to you to mince your words?" she asked cheerfully, in too good a mood to be bothered that he doubted her.

"Nope."

After Central Park, they'd dropped Coco off with Alvin, who'd declared the dog "just the thing" to take his mind off the ringing in his ears that, according to him, was either tinnitus or a brain tumor, and he was leaning toward the latter.

Since they had time to kill before the first jazz set of the night, Violet had dragged Cain on a tour of some of Midtown's highlights. The library. Grand Central. Bryant Park.

He hadn't exactly gushed over the experience, but neither had he complained. Much.

She'd even been able to coax out a few details of his life over their pasta dinner. She now knew that he grew up in a small town on the bayou, but currently lived in a small studio in the French Quarter, owned a motorcycle, and hated cauliflower.

The conversation had been mostly one-sided and exhausting, but it had all been worth it when they'd finally gotten to the jazz club that evening. The pleasure on Cain's face at the first strums of the bass had done funny things to her stomach.

"Is Edith a jazz fan too?" he asked, and she thought she heard a note of hope there, as though he thought it might be something he and his grandmother had in common.

She hated to disappoint him, but she wouldn't lie. "Not really. She doesn't mind it, but she won't seek it out either."

"Then who introduced you to it? Forgive me if I thought you were more of an *adult hits* kind of listener."

"I like all kinds of music," she said. "But jazz is a family love. My grandfather actually played at some of the local clubs back in the day. Sax."

"No kidding."

She took a bite of pizza and nodded. "He died when I was little. Kindergarten. But he passed the love onto my dad, as well as dozens of really great albums. When *he* died . . ." Violet shrugged. "I guess it was a way to connect to that side of my family. My grandma wasn't *quite* the fan I am, but she always loved when I put on Coltrane or Mellé . . ."

She fell silent as she chewed, and for a moment they walked side by side without saying a word as snowflakes whispered around them.

"A lot of death in your story, Duchess. Grandfather. Parents. Grandmother . . ."

She picked at a piece of crust on her plate. "Yeah. But plenty of joy too. I'm lucky in a lot of ways."

Cain stared at his pizza for a minute, then set it on the plate without taking another bite.

"What about you?" she asked. "Where'd your jazz obsession come from?"

"It's not as old as yours. After my mom died, I needed a change of scenery. I moved from the middle of nowhere to New Orleans. I lived in a shithole with two roommates I barely knew. One of them played sax and invited me one night to tag along to his set. I did, and I just . . ."

"Fell in love?" she finished for him.

He smiled a little. "Don't romanticize it, Duchess."

"Why not? Jazz *is* romantic."

He shook his head and took a bite of pizza. "Yeah. Sure. Fine. I fell in love."

"Have you ever been in love for real? With a woman, I mean?" Violet didn't mean to stop walking, but somehow they'd come to a halt, facing each other on the quiet, early morning Harlem sidewalk.

"No," he said without hesitating.

"Ah. I get it. Too tough and strong to do something as silly as falling in love?" she teased.

He didn't smile back. "Not quite like that."

"Then what?" She was surprised by how much she wanted to hear his thoughts. And uneasy about how much she *liked* the fact that he'd never been in love.

His gaze fixed on a point just over her shoulder, the wind pulling some of his hair out of his ponytail, the snowflakes sticking to his beard just for a moment before melting.

"As a general rule, I try to avoid doing stupid shit."

"Falling in love isn't stupid."

His eyes came back to hers. "Speaking from personal experience?"

Violet swallowed at the uncomfortable reminder of Keith, at the even stronger discomfort of realizing she hadn't thought about him all night. But now, she was suddenly very aware that she was out with another man at 1 a.m. They weren't alone—there was no such thing in New York City. There were always cars, people, sirens.

But the snow dusting the roads and sidewalks created a sort of fairy-tale land that made her feel alone.

Not alone. With Cain.

"Well?" he said.

She let out a nervous laugh. "For someone who thinks falling in love is brutal business, you're certainly curious about the details."

"And you're certainly evasive."

"Fine, I love Keith, and no, I don't think love is stupid," she said a little stubbornly. "Happy now?"

His gaze narrowed, and he stepped closer, hand lifting toward her face.

Violet's breath caught in her throat, then released again, when his paper napkin scraped roughly over her chin, and he held it up for her to see. Violet tried valiantly not to grimace in embarrassment at the streak of neon orange pizza grease that had been smeared on her chin.

They began walking again, their footsteps muffled by the snow.

"No," Cain said curtly.

She glanced up, puzzled. "No, what?"

"No to your question." He didn't look her way, his tone deceptively bored. "No. I wouldn't say I'm happy now."

Ten

Silverware scratched lightly over delicate china plates. A sound that generally indicated a dinner party gone horribly wrong, that the conversation wasn't just boring, it was nonexistent.

At *this* dinner party, however, the silence was a vast improvement over the conversation that had preceded it.

Dinner *party*, perhaps, was misleading. *Party* implied a good time among people who liked one another, or were at least capable of faking it. This was a five-course nightmare starring Cain and Keith having some sort of masculine showdown, with Edith and Violet as annoyed spectators.

"So, Cain," Keith finally broke the silence from his seat beside Violet. "You said you worked in distribution?"

Oh, here we go.

"Yup." Cain didn't look up from his steak au poivre,

which Violet was relieved to see he was eating with the correct fork, if not exactly in the Continental style of holding silverware that was generally favored among their circle.

"He's a part owner, actually," Violet said.

Everyone, including Cain, gave Violet a startled look.

She shrugged, refusing to feel embarrassed, and took a bite of potato. "I looked it up."

Cain stared at her a moment longer, assessing, then glanced back at his plate, seemingly more annoyed than flattered.

"Vi, did Cain tell you he came by the office today?" Keith asked over his wineglass, apparently deciding to skip right over any evidence that Cain Stone might be successful back in Louisiana.

"He didn't mention it," Violet said, wiping her lips. Edith had, though. The older woman had texted Violet yesterday to let her know she had a day off from "Cain duty." The phrase had irked Violet. The man didn't need a babysitter, and a grown man shouldn't be anyone's *duty*.

Though, despite her irritation at Edith's choice of words, Violet had also been relieved. She'd relived Monday evening, with its late-night jazz session and spontaneous pizza-on-the-sidewalk a few times too many. And no matter how often she had told herself that it had just been two strangers with a common goal, the fluttering feeling she got every time she replayed the day in her head made the whole episode feel a lot more like a date.

And one that she'd enjoyed far too much given that she and Keith had an understanding of sorts. Guilt was gnawing even harder this evening, with Keith's arm draped around the back of her chair. The casual, possessive gesture was unlike him, but she told herself maybe a bit of proprietary body language on his part was a good thing. Maybe it would ignite the old spark she'd felt in the earliest days of their relationship.

She'd told Cain she loved Keith. Maybe if they *acted* the part, it would feel more . . . true.

"And, what'd you think of the office?" Keith asked Cain impatiently. "Probably a little overwhelming."

Violet closed her eyes in frustration, wishing Keith would do his part to be a little more appealing.

Cain took a sip of water. "*Overwhelming*'s not the word. I grew up with gators living in my backyard. Wing tips are pretty tame by comparison."

Ignoring this, Keith looked over at Violet, letting the backs of his fingers brush over the nape of her neck as he addressed her. "Cain's office is one of the biggest, save for Edith's and my own. Right on the corner with a hell of a view."

"Keith," Edith said calmly, not looking up from her plate as she spoke for the first time in several minutes. "If you're going to swing your *thing* around, please do it somewhere other than at my table."

Violet lifted a napkin to her lips to hide her grin and heard Alvin let out a low chuckle from the kitchen. Even Cain gave his grandmother an admiring half smile.

"I'm just saying," Keith said, sounding petulant. "Cain's sudden ascendance probably grates on some of the old-timers. They've been loyal to the company for years, and he comes in with no business experience—"

"No *corporate office* experience," Edith clarified. "As Violet pointed out, he has plenty of business experience in his own right."

"Whatever. People are probably pissed," Keith said, sounding so sulky that Violet was a little embarrassed for him.

"So far, you're the only one in a snit about it," Edith said, pushing away her plate. "Everybody else seems to be too focused on their work to care about which office Cain takes."

Violet braced for Keith to continue whining, but he apparently decided to finally read the room. He looked around, and Violet saw him taking in Cain's indifference, Edith's icy challenge, Violet's silent plea to *shut up already.*

Keith sat up straighter, removing his hand from Violet's chair, and seemed to transform back into his usual charming self.

"Forgive me," he said to the group. "My upstairs neighbors threw a hell of a birthday bash last night. I didn't sleep as well as I usually do, and I'm never at my best when I don't get my sleep. Violet knows," he said, giving her a wink. At least that's what she thought it was. Keith had never winked at her before, and the gesture didn't look particularly natural, so it was possible he just had something in his eye.

She felt herself blush at his unsubtle insinuation, though she wasn't sure if the blush was due to her intimate life being discussed at the dinner table, or because it felt like a lie.

Or because she felt Cain's gaze on her, and the mere eye contact gave her far more butterflies than Keith's hand against her neck had moments ago.

Keith shifted his attention back to Cain. "I hear you have a call with the Tokyo team next week. I'd love to sit in on that. I've been working on expanding that market, and I'd hate to lose progress because we have a potential change in leadership."

Cain's only response was to shove back his chair, stand, and leave the room without a word.

There was a stunned silence that Keith broke with a laugh. "Well, Violet. Guess you and he haven't hit the manners portion of your lessons yet, huh?"

"Nor, apparently, yours," Violet said coolly. She wiped her mouth and glanced at Edith. "Excuse me for a moment, please."

She stood and followed Cain before she could think how that would look to Edith and Keith. Before she could even register *why* she was doing it.

"For God's sake, Keith," Edith said crisply. "I'm not asking you to be his best friend, just to treat him with respect . . ."

Violet stepped out of the dining room and headed toward the front door, hoping she could catch Cain before he stormed out of Edith's house.

Her footsteps faltered at the sound of music, though, and instead of going to the front door, she turned to the sitting room near the front of the brownstone. It was a small room, not used as often as the main parlor, as the expanse of windows made it too hot in the summer, too cold in the winter.

It also had limited seating, as the majority of the room was taken up by a piano.

A piano that Cain Rhodes knew how to play. Quite well.

His back was to her as she stood in the doorway, listening as he played an unfamiliar song, something that managed to be both upbeat and jazzy, and yet somehow also just a touch melancholy.

She waited until the song slowed to the end before speaking, her voice soft. "All that talk about jazz, and yet somehow you never mentioned you played."

Cain's hands froze over the keys at the sound of her voice before resuming their playing, slightly lighter than before. "You're hardly one to talk." He glanced up briefly. "How is it that earlier when Keith asked what sort of music I liked, he replied to my response by declaring he didn't know anyone who listened to jazz?"

She shifted in the doorway. "Your point?"

"Your man should know what sort of music you listen to, Duchess."

Your man.

The phrase was uncomfortable in a way she didn't feel like exploring.

She stepped farther into the room. "You took lessons?"

For a moment he said nothing, merely played on. "My mom played. We didn't have enough money for a bed for me or for birthday gifts or new clothes. But she'd have rather died than sell the upright she inherited from her grandmother."

Violet stepped closer, pulled in by the music. The man. "She taught you?"

"I guess. More felt like I just always knew how to play."

"Where's that piano now?"

"You ask a lot of questions, Duchess."

Violet was right behind him now, watching his fingers move over the keys, feeling a little wistful at his effortless skill. "I always wanted to play. I took lessons for a few years, but I guess I didn't want it bad enough, because I hated to practice. The only song I ever mastered was 'Heart and Soul.' My mom and I used to play it, over and over, because I couldn't get enough."

For a long moment Cain said nothing in response. When he did reply, it wasn't with words. He shifted slightly on the bench to his left. Making room for her.

She sat beside him, her back to the piano, as he transitioned to something more jazzy, more upbeat. But also not quite like anything she'd heard in jazz clubs. It was moodier somehow. Sultry.

"Sorry about in there," she said quietly, tipping her head toward the dining room.

He didn't stop his playing. Didn't respond.

"Keith can be . . ." She sighed. "He's struggling. He's put a lot of himself into the company, and it's hard for him to have an outsider come in and take a position he thinks should be his."

Cain's eyes flicked up for the briefest of moments. "That's not what he should be possessive of."

Violet didn't reply. Couldn't. But neither did she look away. A mistake. His fingers still moving over the keys, he slowly tilted his face toward hers. She became all too aware that piano benches were built for one and that they were hip-to-hip, their faces just inches from each other.

All week she'd been trying to figure out how to convince him to shave his beard. Up close, she realized she didn't want him to. Not until she knew its texture, not until she knew how it would feel.

He held her gaze for only a second longer before looking back down at the piano.

"You still play 'Heart and Soul'?"

Violet told herself she was relieved for the change in subject. "No. Not really. I'm sure I'd still remember how. There's an out-of-tune piano at my place, but . . ."

No one to play with.

He must have heard what she didn't say because he transitioned seamlessly from the jazz to something far more familiar. Violet smiled when she recognized it.

The bass, secondo part of "Heart and Soul."

Cain didn't say a word as he played the monotonous chords over and over, but nudged her lightly with his elbow.

Violet hesitated a moment, unable to put her finger on whatever she was feeling. She felt strangely on the cusp of something, though she didn't know what.

Cain didn't rush her or nudge her again. He simply played his part. Over and over. Waiting.

It's just a song, Violet.

But it felt bigger than that.

She lifted her right hand and placed her fingers on the keys, waiting until the top of the measure to begin.

As the two parts came together in a bright, familiar melody, she smiled. There was something so cheerful and pure about the simple, slightly awkward part she was playing atop his steady, lower notes. Her fingers were a little bit stiff, out of practice from years of disuse, but they still knew what to do, a flood of childhood memories rushing back, sweet and poignant.

Violet played the last notes, regretting that it was over so soon, but again, Cain seemed to sense what she didn't say. He kept right on playing his part, unwavering and grinning, Violet joined in again from the top. She played with confidence this time, her fingers a little looser, her smile a little wider.

The sound of a throat clearing in the doorway had her fingers missing a note, the pretty song screeching to a discordant halt. Cain played a few more notes before stopping too, albeit more gracefully, on his own terms.

Violet pivoted on the piano bench, embarrassed to see they had an audience. Alvin looked delighted. Edith looked pleased and a little bit glassy eyed.

Violet shifted her attention to Keith, looking prissy and irritated. He extended a hand to Violet. "Vi. Come on. Cheesecake for dessert. Your favorite."

It wasn't.

Nor had Keith even looked her way as he spoke, all of his attention on Cain, his speculative look taking on an edge.

Oblivious, or indifferent, to Keith's scrutiny and the tension in the room, Cain stood abruptly. "Thanks for dinner, Edith."

"You're leaving?" his grandmother asked in surprise, her crestfallen expression tugging at Violet's heart. "Keith's right, we have cheesecake."

"Save me a piece." Cain's voice was kinder than Violet would have expected, but he still didn't hide his intention to leave.

"Where's the fire?" Keith asked, stepping aside as Cain made to exit the room.

"No fire," Cain said in a bored tone. "Just a date."

"A date! That's wonderful," Edith said, clearly pleased at the prospect that Cain might be putting down roots long enough to enter the New York dating scene. "Someone I know? Violet, is this something you set up?"

No. No, it definitely was not.

Before she could identify the root cause of the sudden knot in her stomach, though, Cain was gone.

Eleven

⌒〜

a few days after the dinner party, Violet awoke to a typically curt text from Cain.

Duchess. My place, 11 a.m. Toto can come.

Because it was more command than invitation, Violet
replied with a corresponding level of politeness:

Fine.

He surprised her by replying. Tiring of your duties already?
Told you you wouldn't last a week.

It's been two weeks. Violet shot back. And if you need
something, maybe you should ask your DATE.

Cain, perhaps wisely, didn't respond to that one.

At ten fifty-nine, Violet knocked on Cain's door, her
spare key at the ready. She might have been amenable to
helping him, but she wouldn't *wait* for him if he was busy
entertaining another overnight guest.

It was freezing outside, so she waited exactly ten seconds after her knock before inserting her key into the lock. In twenty degrees, her nylons didn't do much to cut the wind chill.

Her wrist had just started to twist when the front door opened, and Cain gave her a knowing look. "Continuing your life of crime, I see."

"Still struggling to master the basics of dressing, I see," she retorted, and looked around him. "Any houseguests I should be prepared for?"

"Not yet, but the day is young."

She waited impatiently for him step aside so she could enter, but he merely stood his ground, as though to say *make me.*

"Do you want me to come in or not?" Violet said.

"I'm not sure." He rubbed his neck. "You look cranky."

"*I* look cranky? *Your* name should be in the thesaurus under *brooding.*"

He braced his arm on the doorjamb and leaned toward her slightly. "Thought women liked *brooding.*"

"Obviously some of them must," Violet said a little testily. "Based on your busy social life."

Cain smirked and leaned a bit closer. "Ah, so that's why you're cranky. What, you can have a boyfriend, but I can't go on a date?"

"New plan," Violet said. "Let's not concern ourselves with each other's romantic endeavors."

Since he was still smirking and blocking her way, Violet reached out to shove him.

Her palms collided with firm abs, her fingers brushing bare skin as Cain hissed out a breath. Touching him had been a mistake. Lifting her gaze to his even more so. His smirk was gone, and his usual scowl had an extra layer of smolder.

He was right. Women *did* like brooding.

Violet jerked her hands back.

"Where's Toto?" Cain asked, shutting the door behind her.

"*Coco* had a date with Alvin. And she hates the cold." Violet shrugged out of her coat and started to hang it on the creepy giraffe coatrack, only to realize it wasn't there.

She pointed at the empty space. "Where'd the coat-rack go?"

"Sold it," he said, running a hand through his mussed hair. It was loose around his shoulders this morning, instead of in its usual knot at the nape of his neck.

"Sold it?" she repeated. "Why?"

Cain shrugged. "It was weird. I didn't like it, and it was mine to sell."

Walking farther into the home, Violet realized the coat-rack wasn't the only thing he'd gotten rid of. Walls once covered in strange, modern paintings were bare. A sideboard shaped like a cluster of grapes was gone from the entryway.

She stepped into the kitchen and living area and drew up short. The living room was completely empty, the kitchen

packed up into moving boxes. She turned to Cain for explanation.

"Coffee?" he asked, ignoring her questioning look and
nodding to the French press on the counter. One of the few
things that hadn't been packed.

"Where's your furniture?" Violet demanded.

"New Orleans."

She gave him an impatient look.

"If you're referring to *Adam's* furniture, I sold it."

"All of it? The upstairs furniture too? Where will you
sleep?"

"Not under this roof a minute longer than I have to."

Regret stabbed low in Violet's stomach, but she kept her
voice level. "Throwing in the towel, hmm? Hightailing it
back to New Orleans?"

"What?" His head snapped up. "How'd you get there?"

"It's a logical conclusion. You said your furniture was
back in New Orleans, and you've made no secret of how
much you hate it here."

"What do you want, daily confirmation and updates on
my transformation into a stuffy prick?"

"*What* transformation?" she asked. "From where I'm standing, you're as stubborn and difficult as you were on day one."

"Now who's throwing in the towel?" he asked, handing
her a coffee cup. "Finally giving up on me? Decided I'm a lost
cause?"

Something about the way he said it gave her pause.

Finally giving up on me? As though he *expected* her to give up on him. As though he was used to people quitting on him.

Suddenly, rather desperately, she wanted to show him otherwise, though she stayed deliberately cool, since she knew that any suspicion on his part at being pitied would backfire.

"You're not getting rid of me that easily," she said, blowing on the steaming coffee. "So are you going to tell me why you demanded my presence here, or . . . ?"

"Right." He dragged a hand over his face, and she noticed he looked exhausted. "I need a place."

"A place," she repeated.

"A house. Condo. Apartment. Whatever you guys call it in this godforsaken city. A rental," he added. "Something I can leave behind if I have to."

If I have to.

The caveat was interesting, and Violet narrowed her eyes. "Something's changed."

"Oh, God," he muttered, sipping his coffee. "I should have known you'd make it all weird."

"Weird or not, I'm right," she said confidently. "You're not indifferent anymore, no matter how hard you try to be. You're *falling* for it."

"Okay, get out," he said, though it was without heat, and he didn't move. "And what do you mean *it?*"

"The whole package. The city. The grandmother. The job."

He grunted.

"I went to church with Edith on Sunday," Violet continued. "She said you're showing up at the office earlier, and more often. Asking more questions. You want the job."

"Don't make it into a whole thing."

She said nothing, sensing that there was more, and sure enough, he rolled his shoulders with impatience, but continued. "Let's just say that for a company that has the word *International* in the name, their global operations are a mess. They're running the business on state-of-the-art tech, built on processes that are thirty years old."

"And that interests you," she said as she searched his face. It was a statement, not a fact. She could see he was intrigued. He didn't *want* to care, but he did.

"It's what I'm good at," he said in a clipped tone that indicated it was all he was going to say about the matter. "So. Are you going to help me find a new place or not?"

"Sure, okay," Violet said after a moment. "But why? This one is free."

"I don't want free. I want *my* place. Even if it wasn't *his*, I'd hate it. It's cramped and dark. The neighbors are snobs."

"I'm a neighbor," Violet pointed out.

"Exactly."

"Okay," she said, tapping her lips. "So you're looking for an area where the neighbors are more like you. How about the Bronx Zoo?"

He poured himself more coffee, topped her up. "How long you been saving that comeback?"

"It came to me just now," she said, feeling rather proud of herself.

Cain rolled his eyes, but he was smiling.

"Meatpacking District doesn't suck," Cain said after a moment.

The naming of a specific neighborhood surprised her, not because of the neighborhood itself but because he'd done his homework. She was more certain than ever that Cain's attitude had changed over the past couple of weeks. No longer did he seem poised to hop in a cab to LaGuardia for the first flight back to Louisiana at the soonest possible moment.

"Meatpacking District," she mused. "I see that for you."

"Well, thank God. I've been on the edge of my seat awaiting your approval."

She arched an eyebrow. "Awfully sarcastic for a man who needs my help finding a broker."

"A broker?"

"New York's word for a real estate agent," Violet explained. "And you definitely need one."

She pulled out her phone. "I know someone. I'll set something up for next weekend, maybe—"

"Today. I want to find a place today."

"And I want hair and skin like Jennifer Aniston," Violet

said, her attention on her phone. "We all have our delusional pipe dreams."

"I'm serious. Have them set it up. Today. Please," he added a bit gruffly.

She looked up in surprise at the unexpected politeness that sounded a bit like a plea. "I'll see what I can do. *If*," she added, "you put on a shirt."

"Deal," he said, surprisingly affable as he set his mug behind him on the counter. "Are there specific instructions on what I should wear, or am I allowed to choose?"

She looked up. "Okay, I know that's sarcastic, but if you think I won't jump at the chance to pick out an outfit for you . . ."

He winced at the word *outfit* as she'd known he would and retreated upstairs before she could make good on her threat.

A few minutes later, he came back down, both arms lifted as he pulled his hair into the usual knot at the back of his head.

She tilted her head and studied him. "Have you scheduled a haircut yet?"

"No."

"Do you want me to schedule one?"

"No."

"Fine," she said with a shrug, since she was rapidly learning to pick her battles with the man. And, his long hair was growing on her. "Does Edith know you're moving?"

He said nothing.

"You should have told her about selling Adam's stuff," Violet said gently. "He was her son. There may have been things she wanted."

He picked up the coffeepot and disposed of the used grounds. "What makes you think I didn't tell her?"

Because you're generally an ass when Edith's name comes up.

"Any update from the broker?" he asked, jerking his chin toward her phone before Violet could press the Edith matter further.

"Yes, but only because Kimberly is doing me a personal favor, so if you've got *any* charm stored away beneath all the crust, now would be a good time to go digging for it."

The corner of his mouth tilted up in a semi-smile. "Crust, huh?"

"Oh, sorry. *Brooding.* Anyway, we've got an appointment for a place in Meatpacking in an hour and a half. It's the soonest Kimberly could get us in."

"Fine. You eat breakfast?"

"Yes."

"Yogurt?"

"Yes."

"Doesn't count. Let's get real breakfast." He walked to a pile of coats draped over a stack of moving boxes. Violet watched his hand reach for his old leather bomber, then hesitate. He grabbed the wool coat instead. For the life of her, Violet couldn't figure out if she was pleased or bothered by the fact that he'd chosen the Manhattanesque style over his usual.

"I'm not going back to that diner," she said.

"Why not?" He pulled on the coat. "You liked the diner."

"I did not."

"You did so."

She scratched her nose in irritation. He was correct. "Fine. Let's go to the diner."

To rob him of the opportunity to gloat, Violet purposely did not look at him as she marched toward the front door.

He grabbed her hand as she passed, pulling her to a halt, then abruptly released her as though the contact unnerved him.

"Hey." He cleared his throat and didn't quite meet her eyes. "Thank you."

"For?"

"Helping me. I haven't exactly been great to you."

Violet could only stare at him. "Seriously? *You haven't exactly been great to me?* That doesn't even begin to summarize what you've been."

"And yet, you're here," he murmured, his dark gaze dropping to her mouth, lingering just a bit too long. "Awful as I am, you keep coming back. I wonder why that is."

Violet swallowed, the sound audible. "Because Edith asked. Of course."

"Of course," he repeated, his brown eyes lifting to hers.

She could tell he didn't believe it was the whole truth.

Violet didn't quite believe it herself.

Kimberly had declared it a New York miracle: Cain was going to rent the first apartment they'd toured.

Not that he'd said as much yet, but Violet knew he liked the loft. It was obvious from the thoughtful way he assessed the open living space as though mentally planning where to put the television, and that he'd yet to grumble.

He wandered upstairs to check out the bedroom, and Violet stayed back with Kimberly. Violet was a little surprised by how much *she* loved the place. As a lifelong Upper East Sider, the trendy neighborhood known as the Meatpacking District was relatively unfamiliar to her. Aside from attending a few birthday dinners over the years, she'd always had a hard time getting past this neighborhood's origins: *literal* meatpacking. As in slaughterhouses and the whole deal.

Not exactly a romantic history.

But even she had to admit that, as with most areas of New York City over the decades, the neighborhood had reinvented itself rather compellingly. The area was now mostly known for its exclusive nightclubs, posh restaurants, and trendy designer shops, though she knew none of that was what appealed to Cain.

There was an unstructured spontaneity to the area that was the complete opposite of Violet and Edith's beloved

Upper East Side. Instead of ornate building facades, marble foyers, and tidy parks, the Meatpacking District was all about brick, angled streets, a modern industrial aesthetic.

The loft they were touring in particular was about as opposite from Adam's brownstone as was possible while still being in the same city. The space was smaller, but it *felt* bigger. Instead of being long and skinny with multiple separate rooms, the space was one enormous open area, with a metal spiral staircase leading up to a loft.

According to Kimberly, until its recent renovation, it had been used as a storage facility. The floors were original hardwood, with just enough scuff to give the place an inviting "make yourself at home" vibe. The exposed brick walls gave the place warmth, the high ceilings gave it openness, and the brand-new appliances in the kitchen definitely didn't hurt either.

There was a wine chiller built into the cabinets, a warming oven, and an enormous granite island that would easily fit at least four barstools.

"Doesn't this just beg for a gorgeous cheese board and a glass of Barolo?" Kimberly asked Violet, sliding her hand over the counter with a wistful look.

"I'm more of a pinot grigio girl myself, but I could do a serious wine-and-cheese night here," Violet said.

"Sometimes I think I have the most torturous job ever," the perky redhead said, tucking a shoulder-length curl behind her ear. "I'm a Brooklyn girl through and through, but when I see places like this, I wonder if maybe it wouldn't hurt to pick up a lotto ticket every now and then."

At the reference to money, Violet bit the inside of her lower lip. It'd been impossible to miss Kimberly and Cain's frank discussion about the monthly rent. Since Violet had inherited her grandmother's home, she didn't know much about rent prices, but if the amount had seemed uncomfortably astronomical to her, she imagined it had to to Cain as well.

"Will you excuse me? I'm dying to see the upstairs," Violet told Kimberly, who was astute enough to know when to hang back.

Violet set her purse on the counter and reluctantly headed to the stairs. Ogling Cain's future kitchen for its wine-and-cheese potential was one thing. Seeing where he'd put his bed was a whole other thing. One she worried would keep her up at night.

The staircase was not exactly stiletto friendly, so she gripped the railing firmly as she made her way to the second level.

"*Oh*," she said in surprise when she got to the top. The downstairs had plenty of windows that mostly looked out at the surrounding buildings, creating a very urbane feel. The second floor cleared all of that, though, and had an unobstructed view of the Hudson River.

Cain stepped out of a walk-in closet, shoving his hands into his jean pockets when he saw her. "Well. What do you think?"

"I think you use this as the bedroom area," she said, gesturing to the room, then pointing to a smaller area, separated
by a half wall. "And that would make for a great office or
seating area."

"A seating area? For what?"

"Reading." She walked into the space in question. "A big,
comfy chair there. A great lamp. A table for your beer, coffee,
whatever. A bookshelf there," she pointed to the corner, then
looked over at him. "You said you liked to read."

"I did," he said, giving her a thoughtful look. "What do
you think about the place in general?"

"I think you're the one who'll be living here, so what
really matters is what *you* think."

He exhaled and looked around. "I think I can breathe
here."

"And you can't at Adam's? Or Edith's?"

Cain shook his head. "I always feel like I'm going to
break shit. Even the fucking doorknobs feel fragile and fancy
and—"

"Not like *you*," she said, finishing his sentence.

He shrugged.

"I can see that," she said, wandering toward the upstairs
bathroom, then coming up short in the doorway. "Holy—"

"Yeah." He came up behind her. "It's nearly as big as the
bedroom."

It was an exaggeration, but it *was* a big bathroom, especially by city-living standards. The floor was a dark slate that

she vaguely remembered Kimberly mentioned was heated. There was a dual sink on the vanity, a stunning copper claw-foot tub, *and* a walk-in shower in the same dark slate as the floors.

She thought of her own bathroom at home, which was cramped and a little bit fussy, with a pale pink shower curtain, a pedestal sink with barely enough room for her toothbrush, and out-of-date wallpaper. Thought of how she had accepted it as is, without question, without wondering if it fit her, or if she even liked it.

Which she didn't, Violet realized a bit uncomfortably.

She understood all too well what Cain had meant about being able to breathe in this apartment. She felt it too, and for a disorienting moment, she had the strangest sense that *she* belonged here as well.

Not just in this bathroom, but in this home, with—

Him?

No. *No.* It was just regular old house envy, she told herself as she stepped backward in panic. This was shiny and new; hers was tired and old. That was the only reason she felt an aching sense of rightness.

But when her back collided with Cain's chest, his hand resting on her hip to steady her as she wobbled a bit in her stilettos, she couldn't *quite* convince herself it was the only reason.

"Easy, Duchess," he murmured, his breath warm as it ruffled her hair.

Violet closed her eyes, her heart pounding, trying to shove away the aching sense of belonging, as though this was where she was meant to be. Here, in this modern apartment, far from Park Avenue pretension, away from Keith and his polished indifference, away from the ghosts of her past that she had let define her for far too long.

Cain's grip shifted slightly, his fingers warm and firm against her hip, tightening slightly in a way that felt almost reflexive. Possessive.

She wanted to lean back into him, let his solid strength support her. An even stronger, more dangerous urge overtook that one. She wanted to turn around. To set her hand on his jaw, to test the texture of his beard, to let it stir her imagination in a more erotic direction.

Violet's eyes snapped open in panic. What was she *doing*?

She quickly stepped away from him, and his hand dropped back to his side.

"It's a pretty great place," she said, her voice just a little too loud. She turned back to him, feigning indifference, as though nothing had just passed between them.

Cain didn't seem as game to pretend there wasn't an inconvenient amount of electricity between them. His gaze was hot and thunderous as his eyes moved quickly down her body. He closed them for the briefest of moments, and when he opened them, they were back to his usual guarded nonchalance.

"Yeah. Pretty great."

"Are you going to apply?"

"Might as well. I can't imagine liking anything else better, and the sooner I can get out of Adam's place, the better."

He started to turn away, and Violet remembered the reason she'd come up here in the first place. She extended a hand to stop him. "Okay, I have to ask you something."

"Shoot."

Violet swallowed. "This is awkward, but . . . can you afford the rent? I know Edith gave you credit cards for the new clothes and living expenses, but . . ."

"I can."

"Oh," she said a little awkwardly when he didn't expand further. "Great."

He rubbed his knuckles along his jawline, looking frustrated and conflicted.

"Adam left me some money," he said finally. "A shit ton of it. Separate from the CEO job, just . . . no strings attached."

Violet stared at him, trying to process this. "Wait, so . . . even without you taking over the company, you're still . . ."

"Rich as fuck."

She was getting used to his language and didn't so much as flinch. Probably because she was too busy trying to sort through her surprise and confusion.

"So if you're already independently wealthy, why—"

"Put myself through this bullshit?" he said. "Because I want to earn it, Duchess. Something you wouldn't understand."

"Right," she said softly. "All I had to do was lose my entire family to get my wealth, right?"

Cain cursed under his breath. "That's not what I meant."

"Then you shouldn't have said it," she said, brushing by him.

"Duchess." He touched her elbow.

She shook him off but turned around to glare at him. "What?"

She waited. His jaw worked, as he looked torn between regret and stubbornness.

When it became clear he wasn't going to say anything, Violet shook her head. "Keep at it, Cain. Keep pushing away the one person who's trying to help you, keep hurting my feelings every chance you get. Just know that one of these days, you're going to push too hard. And I won't come back."

Twelve

"You see what I mean?" Alvin asked triumphantly. "It's glaucoma."

Violet pulled back from staring intently at the older man's eyes. "To be honest, I don't know what I'm looking at. Aren't there tests for glaucoma? You know, by actual doctors?"

He scowled. "Yes. But I'm beginning to have my doubts about Western medicine."

She nodded in understanding, even as she mentally translated: he *had* taken a glaucoma test, and it had come back negative.

"Well, let's keep an eye on it. Pun intended. We'll give it a week, and if it's still bugging you, we can start looking at alternative treatments. That okay?"

He beamed at her. "You really are the dearest. And you'll

be pleased to hear that my bowel movements have returned to normal." Alvin made an A-OK gesture as he said it, and she made one back.

"Delighted to hear it. Edith in the parlor?" she asked, already moving that direction before he could launch into detail she *really* didn't want to hear.

Edith stood at the sideboard, arranging a large bouquet of white and yellow roses when Violet joined her. "Ah, there you are. I'm so glad you could join me."

"I rarely say no to happy hour," Violet said with a smile. "Especially one of yours. It's been too long since we've caught up."

"It has," Edith said, looking regretful. "Things have been so hectic with Cain—he won't be joining us, by the way."

"A shame," Violet said, lying smoothly. She hadn't had contact with the infernal man since the apartment tour, and the distance had been suiting her just fine.

"White wine okay?" Edith asked, moving from the flowers to the elegant marble wine chiller. She lifted a bottle of Chablis in question, and Violet nodded.

"Truthfully, Violet?" Edith said with a tired sigh as she poured them each a small glass. "I'm glad it's just us today."

"Oh?" Violet asked cautiously, accepting the glass and sitting.

Edith nodded. "I wanted to talk to you alone. Girl talk, I guess they call it?"

"Is everything okay?" Violet asked, a little thrown off by

Edith's mood. "I know I haven't been around to help you as much as usual, but with the Cain thing—"

"Violet." Edith set a hand on hers and took a seat beside her. "Stop. I've missed you, is all."

"Oh!" Violet felt touched, but nonplussed. "I've missed you too."

Edith smiled and sipped her wine. "So, tell me. How have you been?"

Violet blew out a breath, wondering how honest to be. "Let's just say the past couple of weeks have been interesting."

"That they have. But you've made significant progress. Cain's different, isn't he? His wardrobe's noticeably improved. Most importantly, he doesn't snarl at everyone in the office as he did in those first days."

Probably because he's been saving all his snarls for me, and me alone.

"He also seems to like the new apartment he moved into in record time," Edith continued in a thoughtful tone. "I stopped by yesterday to see it. Can't say I'd want to live there myself, but he seemed more relaxed."

"I'm sure he is. It suits him."

Edith was studying her. "You've been there?"

"I helped him find the broker. I hope that's okay."

Edith tilted her head. "Why wouldn't it be okay? I asked you to help him settle into the city."

"Yes, but I know you were probably hoping that it would be in Adam's house."

Edith took another tiny sip of wine. "Perhaps I was hoping that. But I think Cain had the right of it. I think a fresh start is best. For him, and for me."

"How so?" Violet asked, genuinely curious. She loved Edith, but the older woman could be a bit set in her ways. She hadn't even realized *fresh start* was in the woman's vocabulary.

"I suppose I've realized a tiny part of me has been trying to simply insert Cain into the empty space Adam has left. That's partially necessary, if I want him to take over the company, but on a personal level, I suppose I need to give Cain a chance to be Cain. Don't I?"

Spoiler alert: Cain "as he really is" is an ass.

Still, it was a big step for Edith and for her relationship with her grandson. An important one. So Violet nodded encouragingly.

Edith looked down at her glass, seeming fascinated with the liquid, though she didn't take another sip. "May I ask you something? A bit personal?"

"Of course."

Edith looked up, her blue eyes searching Violet's face. "How are things with you and Keith?"

"Keith?" Violet repeated. "He's—we're . . . fine. Same as we've always been. Fine."

Edith looked like she actually *bit* her tongue at that, but she smiled. "I'm glad. It's just, I've realized recently, you and Cain have been spending plenty of time together."

"Because you asked us to," Violet pointed out.

"I did, I did. Though I wonder if perhaps I didn't think that through all the way."

"Meaning?"

"My initial thought when I learned of him was that he was my biological grandson, and here's my adopted grand-daughter, of sorts."

Violet's smile at Edith referring to her as a granddaughter faded at her next words.

"I suppose, in my head, I was thinking of you two as sib-lings."

Violet took an unladylike gulp of wine. She had plenty of thoughts about Cain Stone. *Brother* wasn't one of them.

"Cain's an attractive man," Edith pressed on when Violet said nothing.

"So is Keith," Violet said, more out of knee-jerk loyalty than passionate conviction. Keith was handsome, just not in a way that made her feel hot every time she looked at him.

"Of course. He's very attractive," Edith agreed easily—too easily. "And you know, all this time, I had thought Keith was an excellent partner for you."

"Really?" Violet was surprised. She knew Edith didn't *dislike* Keith, but she'd never exactly gushed about him either.

Edith nodded slowly. "You've experienced so much loss, Violet. And I myself am not getting any younger."

"Edith—"

"No, let me say this," the other woman said, holding up a

hand. "I won't be around forever, and it's been important to me that you'll have someone after I'm gone."

"And you think that someone is Keith?"

Edith hesitated. "I think Keith is steady . . . I think he'd be there."

Physically maybe, Violet thought. But emotionally? In the way that mattered, the way she *wanted*?

"Why are you telling me all of this?" Violet asked warily.

"Well," Edith exhaled. "The thing is, Vi, I'm not so sure I've had the right of it. That isn't easy for me to say, but . . ."

Her voice trailed off, and she got a dreamy expression on her face. "Did you know that when Bernard and I first met, he was a volunteer firefighter?"

"I definitely did not," Violet said, surprised. Bernard Rhodes had been a large, imposing man—something he'd passed on to his grandson—but Bernard has also been polished to the point of stuffy. She had very few memories of Edith's late husband in anything other than a three-piece suit. Even when they'd gone to the Southampton beach home, his polo shirts had been ironed, his shorts perfectly pressed.

"He played in a rock band. Drums. The band—oh, what were they called—the Blue Flames were terrible, absolutely dreadful. Bernard knew it but he loved being a part of it anyway. And he had a little tattoo." Edith smiled. "Right here." Edith reached around and tapped the back of her right shoulder.

"I'm shocked," Violet said with a little laugh. "I had no idea. I feel like I barely knew him!"

"And did you know, Bernard was adamant for quite some time that he wanted nothing to do with the family business. It also took him nearly five years to pop the question," Edith said. "And I was never quite sure he would."

"Five years," Violet repeated. "And you stuck around?"

Edith twisted the wedding ring she still wore and smiled. "One of the few times in my life I bided my time and tried to be patient. I loved him. Even if he'd never asked for my hand, I don't think I'd have stopped loving him, but he was not . . . predictable. He wasn't safe. Not like Jimmy."

"Who the heck is Jimmy?"

"One of my other beaus. We went steady for years before I met Bernard. And for a little bit after. I eventually broke things off when I realized my heart didn't beat quite wildly enough for him, but he kept coming around, promising things Bernard wouldn't. A wedding, a family, a nice house, a predictable income. All the things I wanted."

"So why didn't you say yes?"

The faraway look on Edith's face faded, and she came back to the present, giving Violet a sharp, steady look. "Because I realized there was something I wanted more."

Thirteen

"D o you want to go over the whole silverware thing again?" Violet asked, facing off with a scowling Cain.

They were in his new apartment—his bedroom, to be precise—prepping for a dinner with Edith and two of the most influential Rhodes International board members.

On the surface, it was simply dinner.

In reality, it was more an interview than a social engagement, and Cain's edginess told her he was well aware of this fact.

"Well?" she asked when he stayed stubbornly silent.

"The little knife is for the butter, don't wipe my pits with the finger towel, bread plate's on the left," he said, accepting the dress shirt she handed him. "I forget, though—am I supposed to bray at the table, or no?"

Violet sighed. "Just get dressed. You're going to be late."

"What are you even doing here?" he asked, punching his arm into the sleeve.

"Isn't it obvious? I can't get enough of all this groveling gratitude."

In reality, she was only here because Edith had asked her to help talk him through any questions that might come up.

Though, following her strange conversation with Edith yesterday, she wasn't entirely sure the older woman's insistence Violet come over to Cain's tonight didn't have more to do with matchmaking aspirations than preparing him for the dinner.

And if that was the case, Edith had better start preparing herself to be disappointed. Cain was being *particularly* antagonistic tonight, which was impressive considering his baseline was on the sharp side of prickly.

"Why'd you order me so many damn suits?" he was grumbling.

"It's actually not that many," she said, glancing at the line of garment bags hanging in his closet. "Don't forget, if you get the job, you'll be wearing them daily, or at the very least, every weekday."

"Well now, see, that's the beauty of being head of the company, right? I can wear whatever the hell I want, and it doesn't have to be suits if I don't fucking feel like it."

"Good point," Violet said, unruffled. "I'll just go ahead and see if they make custom dungarees in your size."

"Make sure you get them extra large. Down there, if you know what I mean."

"How could I possibly know what you mean?" She frowned in fake confusion. "You're so subtle and not at all cliché."

Cain had started to button his shirt. "Are you sure about this color?" he asked, glancing down skeptically at the dark blue shirt. "Isn't white more . . . traditional?"

She lifted her eyebrows. "And you *want* traditional?"

He scowled. "This one is shiny."

"It's not shiny, it's—just button it. Unless you're only good at unbuttoning things."

He gave her a look beneath his lashes. "Is that an invitation?"

She ignored his question and went to the bed, where Cain had upended the bags provided by the tailor. "Actually, wait. There's supposed to be undershirts in here. Ah. Here we go."

She picked up a package of white V-necks. "Put one of these on first."

Violet tossed him the package, which he caught one-handed and ripped open with his teeth. She breathed a silent sigh of relief when he pulled the shirt on. It was a little easier to think clearly around the man when he was clothed. Not a lot easier. But a little.

"Does Keith know how often you ogle my bare chest?" Cain asked.

"No. I don't want to embarrass Edith, so I've been keeping it quiet how often you struggle to dress yourself."

"Your comebacks are sharpening. I like it."

"What a relief." She handed him the dress pants. "I'll wait downstairs," she said, starting toward the door.

"Scared, Duchess?"

He asked the question lightly, mockingly. Enough to have her stopping. "Why would I be scared?"

Cain ambled toward her, seeming much less perturbed by his chest than she was. "What would Keith think? You. Here. With me. Like this."

She swallowed but forced herself to give him a bored look. "I'm sure Keith would be concerned that it's taking the better part of half an hour for a grown man to dress himself. In fact, if you want me to call him over, show you how it's done . . ."

His mouth tilted up in the corner with begrudging respect, and she knew she'd won that one.

One–zero, Violet!

Then her stomach dropped as she saw Cain's hand go purposefully to the fly of his jeans. His eyes locked on hers as he flicked open the button with his thumb.

Fine. One–one. A tie.

She turned pointedly around, giving him her back. He snickered, and she heard the sound of denim dropping to the floor, being kicked aside.

As he changed, she pulled the suit jacket off the hanger. She'd selected a dark gray for the evening; less corporate than blue pinstripe, but conservative enough to let the board members know he was taking this seriously.

She hooked a finger under the collar, holding it out for him to grab.

"Well?" he asked a minute later.

Violet turned back around, and her lips parted at the man before her. Recognizable, but . . . not. The suit was fitted to perfection, though it somehow seemed to fit him differently than any other man she knew. Keith went to the gym daily and was well sculpted, but Cain carried his fitness differently. Bigger. Broader. Rougher.

Hotter.

"Good," she said with an awkward nod. "Now, for the tie."

She went to the bed, picked one up.

"No. Hell no. It's pink."

Violet glanced at the tie in her hand. "It's coral."

"Call it whatever you want, I'm not wearing it."

Violet rolled her eyes but set the tie aside and picked up a light blue one off Cain's unmade bed. "Better?"

He lifted a shoulder. "Fine."

Violet handed it to him, noticing the slightest hesitation before he accepted it.

"Do you—know how to tie it?" she asked.

"I'm not that backwater," he snapped. Then hesitated, obviously embarrassed and hating to be so. "It's been a while."

"No problem," she said. "Just loop it over your neck."

She waited until he did so, then stepped closer, lifting her hands to him, then hesitating. "Do you mind? There are probably a million YouTube videos you can watch to teach yourself, but since we're short on time . . ."

"Go for it," he said a bit gruffly.

Violet reached out again, taking both ends of the tie and beginning the process of turning it into a tidy knot.

"You're smiling," he said quietly.

Her gaze flicked up. He was very close. And taking no pains to disguise the fact that he was studying her.

She dropped her gaze back to what her hands were doing. "I was just remembering I used to do this for my dad. He didn't need me to, of course, but I loved being a part of his and my mom's fancy nights out. I can't believe I still remember how, honestly. It's been years."

Violet tightened the knot, which she was pleased to note was perfect, then moved her hands back, making sure the tie was tucked neatly beneath his collar.

Her fingers found the knot at the back of his head, his hair in its usual messy, pulled-back style. Her breath caught, and her fingers lingered, itching with the strangest urge to pull out the band. She'd seen it down around his shoulders only once, but she wanted to again. Wanted even more to explore what it would feel like between her fingers, to find out what he would do if—

Suddenly, his hand was behind her head, his fingers tangling in her hair and tugging backward until her face tilted up to his. The motions were surprisingly gentle, but his voice was harsh. "You can't decide, can you?"

Violet swallowed awkwardly. "What do you mean?"

"Who you want me to be. The perfect, boring creation of your own making, your very own homemade arm candy to show off to your friends. Or the guy from the wrong side of the tracks to scratch that bad boy itch between your legs."

Her lips parted, though she didn't know if it was in surprise, anger, or desire. Perhaps a combination of the three.

His fingers tugged a little more firmly in her hair, and desire abruptly took the lead, followed by a wave of yet another emotion.

Guilt.

"Let me spell it out for you, Duchess," Cain said before roughly pulling her all the way to him and crushing his mouth over hers.

His kiss was carnal. Firm lips deftly coaxed hers open. His tongue slid against hers without apology. The fingers in her hair tightened, even as his free hand roamed at will, molding her hips, her butt, then gliding over her waist until the heel of his hand pressed against the side of her breast, pausing . . .

Lost in a desire so unfamiliar, so all-consuming that she couldn't see straight, Violet made a moaning sound of want and arched against him without thinking. *More!*

Cain pushed her back as abruptly as he'd pulled her forward.

"Any questions?"

"Wh-what was that for?" she asked, confused and more than a little unsteady on her feet.

"To show you I'm not your guy, not in any capacity. I never will be. Now get the hell out of my house."

Fourteen

"Oh my God," Ashley said, in awe after Violet had finished recounting the incident. "You got the grab-and-kiss."

"The what?" Violet asked tiredly as she poured them each a cup of Earl Grey tea. Not her most original Sunday tea moment, but she'd more or less been operating on autopilot since Cain had turned her world upside down with his kiss, only to cruelly reject her seconds later. To say that she hadn't gotten much sleep was an understatement.

"You're obviously not reading the romance novels I keep insisting you try. You know, it's when . . ." Ashley didn't leave her usual spot on the love seat, but mimed grabbing Violet's shoulders and jerking her forward. "Where a guy just *claims* you."

Ashley gave a little shiver of delight at her own description and fanned herself. "There is nothing hotter."

She paused her fanning to accept the teacup and gave Violet a careful look. "Unless it *wasn't* hot . . ."

Violet stirred her tea and said nothing.

"Vi?" Ashley was concerned now. "Was it *violating*? Did he—"

"No," Violet said quickly. "No, it was . . ." Violet relented and sighed. "It *was* hot."

"Damn," Ashley muttered, petting Coco, then picking up one of the Ladurée macarons she'd brought over. "And then he had to ruin it by talking. Why do guys *always* go and do that?"

"It's just as well that he did," Violet said, running a hand over Coco's back as the little dog hopped up into her lap.

"Because of Keith?" Ashley asked.

Violet groaned and slumped slightly in her chair, careful not to dislodge Coco. "Keith. What am I going to do?"

But she already knew. She could not, in good conscience, feel the way she had when Cain Stone kissed her *and* maintain her relationship with Keith. And it wasn't just about her conscience. Even *before* Cain had kissed her, Violet had felt herself waking up to the sense of wanting more. More from her life, and more from the man in her life.

"You kissed Cain back?" Ashley asked gently.

"I don't even know. I guess not *technically*, because it was over so fast." *Too fast.* "But a technicality doesn't change the fact that I liked it."

"So, what's the big deal?" Ashley said loyally. "It's not as though you and Keith are headed toward an engagement or anything."

Violet gave her friend a startled look. "You sound awfully confident about that."

More confident than Violet herself had felt; just a month earlier, she'd assumed that she and Keith were on the path toward marriage. Just a really slow, winding, underwhelming path.

Ashley's eyes went wide in panic. "I'm so sorry, Vi. I thought—I assumed—"

Her friend chewed her lip, then shifted uneasily, and Violet gave her a gentle, but firm look. "Ash."

Her best friend leaned forward to set the teacup down. "Okay, first, I swear to God, I would have told you earlier if I had thought *you* thought Keith was the one."

"Told me what?" Violet knew her friend's expressions enough to brace for bad news.

Ashley puffed out her cheeks, then blew out a breath. "A few months ago, I went to Kristen's birthday party. You, me, and Keith, we were all planning to cab over together, but you had to cancel at the last minute."

Violet nodded. "Right. I had that nasty stomach bug."

"Yep. So, without you, Keith and I had no reason to share the cab. He was already there when I arrived. I . . . I could be wrong, Vi, but he and Erin McVale seemed *super* friendly. And then they left together." Her friend looked agonized. "I didn't want to make assumptions, since it's not like I caught them making out or anything. But they were a little handsy, you know? I just got the feeling . . . maybe they went back to her place. Or his."

Violet rubbed an index finger over the top of Coco's head, waiting to feel something. Anything.

"You're mad," Ashley said on a tortured groan. "I should have told you."

"I'm actually *not mad*," Violet said truthfully. "Not at you, not even at Keith. I'm not anything. But shouldn't I be?"

"Well, if you thought you were going to marry the guy, yeah, Vi. You should be seething in jealousy or anger right now. The fact that you're not . . ."

Violet sighed and confessed fully to her friend. "The other day, I was trying to remember the last time Keith and I had sex. I couldn't. But then it got even worse: I realized I couldn't even remember the last time we'd *kissed* beyond a quick, routine peck.

"And he's never seemed to mind. Or notice. So, I suppose on some level," Violet continued slowly, "I knew he was probably getting it somewhere else. From *someone* else."

"And what about you?" Ashley asked. "*Please* tell me you've gotten some somewhere."

Violet hesitated, then shook her head. She'd never been the casual sex type, and even before she and Keith had cooled off, she'd never felt any real punch of lust that kept her up at night.

"Okay, that's just not right," Ashley was saying. "Thank God Cain's come along, and—"

"I'm not going to sleep with Cain."

"Why the hell not?" Ashley demanded. "You two obviously have chemistry."

I'm not your guy . . . I never will be.

"He doesn't want me. I told you all the stuff he said," Violet replied.

"The stuff he said *after he kissed you.* Actions always speak louder than words, babe, especially when it comes to guys. The kiss is the telling thing, not his words. Though if you want to scrutinize them: that crap about you not being able to decide whether you're falling for your own arm candy creation or you just want to get your rocks off with a bad boy?"

Violet let out a pained laugh. "Yeah. That."

"Garbage," Ashley said decisively, picking up a turquoise macaron, studying it for a moment, then putting the entire thing into her mouth. "It's a classic penile defense system."

"Do I even want to know what that is?" Violet asked skeptically.

Ashley frowned at her like a schoolteacher. "I'm serious on those romance novels, Vi. They'll teach you everything you need to know."

Violet lifted her dog to her face and gave the pup a nuzzling kiss. "Coco, will you remind your Auntie Ashley about that time we wrote her *To Kill a Mockingbird* book report in eighth grade so she could go to the movies with Benny Gould? She owes us the CliffsNotes version of her romance novel learnings."

Ashely gave a smug grin. "For the record, I have no regrets over that morally sketchy favor I asked you for. I got my first kiss thanks to you! And I read *To Kill a Mockingbird* on my own—eventually. Last year."

"Okay, well, I'm thrilled about your first kiss, but I may have just experienced my *last* kiss thanks to you, if you don't help me," Violet said, taking a large gulp of her tea, then setting Coco on the floor and grabbing a cookie. Then two more.

"Okay, fine, but you'd better take notes, because this is crucial stuff," Ashley proclaimed. "So, the penile defense system is when a guy's got it for you bad, but for whatever reason, he doesn't want to want you. So he pushes you away. In other words," Ashley said, scooting over so Coco could claim her favorite corner of the love seat, "Cain is rejecting you before you can reject him. And the fact that he's doing it in such a blunt manner means he's got it *bad.*

"My theory?" Ashley continued, brushing her fingertips together to get rid of the brightly colored crumbs. "As much as Cain wants to convince you that he's a bad guy, I think deep down he's a bit of a straight arrow. He's got a code of conduct he won't breach."

"Um, I really don't think so," Violet said, shaking her head. "I've spent a lot of time with the guy, and nothing about him screams rule follower. And besides, what rule could he possibly think he's breaking?"

Ashley gave her a patient look. "The one where you don't steal another guy's woman. Isn't it obvious, sweetie? He's not going to put himself out there, not as long as he thinks you belong to Keith."

Violet had known for a while now that her romantic history was on the slim side compared to others her age. She'd had a couple of crushes in high school, had gone to prom with a nice boy named Sam, but hadn't actually *truly* had a boyfriend until she'd gone to college. First Michael, who'd ended things when he'd transferred after freshman year. And then Erik, who'd been her whole world until he'd dumped her senior year and started dating someone else a week after.

Since that whopper of a heartache, she'd dated a couple of men very casually, all of whom had simply sort of drifted away when she began seeing Keith without any big confrontation or fireworks.

All of which was to say: if her romantic experience was meager, her *ending* relationships experience was completely nonexistent.

She'd been the dumpee, but never the dump*er.*

That changed tonight.

Nervous as she'd been in the hours leading up to her dinner with Keith, Violet was surprised to realize that she wasn't as jittery and nauseous as she'd expected to be. Instead, she felt almost . . . anticipatory?

Not to say that she was looking forward to it—of course not. She didn't want to hurt Keith. But on some level, Violet also was pretty sure she wouldn't hurt Keith.

Because he didn't love her, not in the way she wanted to be loved. She had no doubt his ego would be stinging by the time she'd said her piece. But his heart? It would be just fine.

As for her own heart, Violet was a bit more concerned. Not that it would be broken the way it had been after Erik had dumped her. But Violet was also very aware that her heart had been safe in Keith's keeping; perhaps that's why it had never belonged, even partially, to Keith in the first place:

She'd known that even if he'd done his worst, it wouldn't have cut deeply, because Violet hadn't *felt* deeply.

And they both deserved a relationship with a bit more skin in the game.

They both deserved to be in love, but it would never be with each other.

"I'm thinking the duck," Keith mused, completely oblivious to her train of thought, as he studied the menu. "What are you getting?"

"The pasta special." She'd decided the second the server had said the words *mushroom cream sauce.*

Keith looked up. "Really? You never get pasta."

"Well, I'm getting it tonight," she said calmly as she

caught the server's eye. "May we have more bread?" she asked.

Violet pointed to a small, empty dish in the center of the table. "Oh, and more of whatever this was."

"Garlic herb butter," the server said with a smile. "Chef specialty. We all joke the secret ingredient is magic, because none of us can seem to re-create it at home."

"Damn," Violet said with a grin. "There go my weekend plans."

The server removed the empty bread basket and butter dish and walked away. Violet glanced at Keith to find him staring at her.

"What?"

"Since when have you said *damn*? Or for that matter, since when have you eaten carbs?"

Since Cain Stone fed me a bite of pancakes in a diner with sticky tables and awful coffee and told me I deserve better than fine. Since we walked through Central Park and ate a pretzel, and watched ice skaters, and enjoyed a day without plan or agenda.

She wasn't breaking up with Keith because of Cain, or at least not only because of Cain. But she was breaking up with Keith because of what she'd learned from the taciturn Louisianan. She'd realized that she was bored with her tidy, safe, never-changing life. Bored with going to the same places, ordering the same food, following the same schedule. Not because she had an issue with routine, but because she wasn't entirely sure she'd even chosen her own routine. She'd simply fallen into it.

Violet wanted more. She wanted to *feel* more, even if that sometimes hurt.

Keith set his menu aside, ironically, more focused on her than she'd ever seen him. And concerned. "Are you okay?"

"I ate some bread, Keith. It's not like I started hearing voices."

He smiled, and there was a touch of pitying condescension in his expression that rankled. "It's the Cain thing, huh? It must be wearing on you. I know it has been on me. Did you know he joined a video conference with London today with no tie and his top button undone?"

Her eyes went wide. "*No.*" Her voice was scandalized. "No tie? What did the FBI say?"

Keith went still, and very slowly set his drink aside. "Okay, Violet. What is going on?"

Violet had played out this conversation with Ashley a handful of times, but sitting across from him now, she ditched the script, skipped all the niceties, and got right down to it.

"I don't want to do this anymore."

Keith, waving around his wineglass in an oblivious motion, said, "Take it up with Edith. I told you from the beginning it was a bad idea."

"I'm not talking about Cain," Violet said calmly. "I mean this—you and me—it isn't working."

He looked more irritated than surprised. "What are you talking about?"

His impatient tone made it easier for Violet to be blunt. "I want to break up, Keith."

This time he *was* surprised.

He said nothing as their server returned with the bread and butter. Violet thanked her, then took her time picking the largest slice and slathering it liberally with the magic butter as Keith continued to stare at her.

Finally, he seemed to gather his thoughts enough to speak, though his chosen words only solidified her decision. "You're breaking up with me," Keith spat. "For some redneck hick."

His laugh was grating and harsh. "You know, I almost want to applaud your initiative, Violet. You think you're going to pull off his transformation, and are betting that *he'll* become CEO, not me. And you'll be there, legs spread, huh?"

"Don't be disgusting," she said calmly. "I'm breaking up with you because we're not in love, Keith. We barely look at each other. We don't talk about things that matter. We haven't had sex in forever."

"Because that's not the sort of relationship you want."

She laughed. "Says who?"

"Says you!" he said, impatient. "I thought . . . I thought this was what you wanted. A companion. I've been that. Haven't I?"

Keith looked utterly befuddled now, and Violet softened her tone.

"To be honest, Keith, I haven't given much thought to what I wanted until now, but I am grateful for your companionship over the years. I just . . . I want more, Keith. Don't you? I think we both deserve it."

"More *what*, Vi? This isn't high school. We can't be making decisions based on whether or not we give each other butterflies and boners. We care about each other, that's what matters. We have the same friends, the same goals . . ."

"I want the butterflies, Keith! And maybe the fact that we're so *same* is part of the problem. I mean, when was the last time we came to a restaurant that wasn't *this* one?"

"But you're ordering pasta," he said a little desperately. "That's different. You can change things up without having to blow them up."

He didn't get it. He would never get it. And that was okay. But it wasn't enough.

"Keith." Violet reached out and took his hand. "Are you in love with me?"

He stared at her for a too-long moment before replying. "Of course."

She smiled because the pause was somehow louder than the words. "No," she said fondly, patting his hand and releasing it. "You're not. I'm not your girl."

Keith's frustration was palpable. "What the hell does that mean? You want my class ring? A letterman's jacket?"

"No. No," she repeated. "I don't want any of that."

Not from you.

"What *do* you want, Violet?"

"I don't know," she said. "But that's what I intend to find out."

Without meaning to, Violet stood up. Keith's mouth dropped almost comically. "You're leaving?"

Apparently, she was.

This hadn't been part of the plan. She hadn't meant to *leave.* But she was acting on instinct, and instinct told her she didn't want to be here right now. Not at this restaurant, not with this man.

Not a minute longer.

She was tired of it all. Tired of his weary tone, as though talking to her was a chore to be endured even as he tried to make her stay. Tired of the fussy restaurants that all looked the same, with their white rose in the center of the white tablecloth and white plates . . . Where was the *color*?

"Enjoy the duck." She bent to pick up her purse and stood up straight. And wasn't it just *sad* that that's the only thing she could think to say to this man, in this moment.

"Violet—" He looked around the restaurant a bit frantically but made no move to get to his feet. Because he didn't want to make a scene. She understood. She understood better than anybody, because a month ago she'd have had the exact same reaction.

And it was the last bit of confirmation she needed that she was making the right choice.

She went around the table and, placing her hand lightly on his shoulder, bent to kiss his cheek. "Goodbye, Keith."

Violet turned and walked away, relieved, but not surprised, when he didn't follow her.

She retrieved her jacket from coat check and stepped into the January night air.

The restaurant was in easy walking distance of her apartment. She started that way and pulled out her cell phone to invite Ashley over to recap the night's events, then remembered her friend was at a work event.

She had other friends she could call, there was an open house birthday party she could stop by, but she wasn't in the mood to field the *where's Keith?* inquiries. Not until she'd had a bit longer to process, and to figure out that particular script.

For the first time in longer than she could remember, Violet paused and asked herself the question Keith had asked.

What *did* she want?

How did she want to spend a Friday night? The first one in a long while where she didn't have standing dinner plans with Keith, or a fundraiser, or a friend's bachelorette party, or a movie night with Edith and Alvin?

A night just for her, when she could do anything she wanted?

Then it hit her, the urge pure and strong. She knew exactly where she wanted to be, somewhere nobody in her life—not even Ashley—ever cared to join her, and tonight, she was just fine with that.

Violet lifted her hand for a taxi. Being a busy Friday night, she had to wait awhile, and by the time she arrived at Columbus Circle, she knew her chances of getting a seat this late, this close to the start of the set, were slim, but she made her way up to the jazz club anyway.

It was one of the swankier clubs in the city, but not a favorite—she preferred the small, crowded ones, packed with people and history. But they had a great trio tonight featuring an up-and-coming female bassist she'd been following.

"All of my tables are taken," the hostess said with an apologetic smile. "But I can squeeze you in at the bar if you just give me a second to ask a couple people to shuffle."

"That would be so great, thank you."

"Sure, just give me a moment," the hostess said, smiling in apology as she picked up the relentlessly ringing phone on her hostess stand.

Violet stepped to the side and scanned the scene, taking in the dimly lit room buzzing with quiet conversation, an employee adjusting the microphone onstage and setting out water bottles for the musicians.

Feeling eyes on her, Violet's gaze swung to her right where a man sat at one of the tiny tables, studying her over a glass of whiskey.

Cain.

He wore a suit, though as Keith had noted derisively, he didn't wear a tie, and Cain had unbuttoned the top two buttons. The blend of formal and casual suited him, she was irritated to see. The man was relentlessly appealing, no matter the attire.

Cain lifted an eyebrow, his shoe shifting beneath the table, and used his foot to gently push out the chair opposite his in silent invitation.

Without registering her intent to move, Violet found herself walking toward him, moth to flame. And when she dropped into the chair, she felt an unexpected sense of comfort.

She hadn't realized just how heavy and *flat* her time spent with Keith felt until it was contrasted with this moment. Here, Violet could simply *be*. She could do whatever she wanted, order whatever she wanted . . .

Be with whomever she wanted.

Violet was still mad at Cain. His punishing kiss, his crass words, his intent to hurt were still fresh in her mind.

But even the anger felt good.

She felt almost crackling. Vibrant. *Alive.*

Here, with him, there was no pressure to keep conversation rolling with inane chatter about the weather or traffic, to not be on constant "awkward silence" patrol.

In fact, other than Violet ordering a sauvignon blanc from the server, they didn't say a word until the musicians were headed up to the stage.

"I was a jerk," he growled suddenly.

Violet glanced at him in surprise. She hadn't guessed he'd be the one to break the silence, nor had she expected an acknowledgment of his boorish behavior.

"Yes," Violet said, holding his gaze steadily, refusing to make this comfortable for him. "You were."

He dipped his chin down in acknowledgment. "I apologize. You didn't deserve it."

"Thank you for that," she said quietly.

Cain lifted a shoulder and turned back to the stage. The silence continued for a few more moments, and this time it was Violet who spoke.

"I broke up with Keith." She announced it casually, in between small sips of mediocre wine.

Cain took his time looking her way again, his eyes seeming to study every nuance of her features.

He looked back at the stage then, rubbing a thumb along his glass as he watched an employee hand a water bottle to the bassist.

When he finally did speak, he never looked away from the stage. "You okay?"

"Yeah," Violet said softly. "Yeah. I'm okay."

And strangely . . . she *was*.

Sitting here listening to jazz with Cain Stone? She was somehow *better* than okay.

Fifteen

The next night, Violet adjusted her grip on the enormous binder and knocked on the front door of Cain's new apartment. She didn't have a key to the new place, and he certainly hadn't offered one, so all she could do was hold her breath and pray he didn't have female company.

When he finally opened the door, there was a flash of something besides surprise in his eyes, but she didn't know what it was and told herself she didn't care.

"Duchess?"

She held out the enormous white binder. "From your grandmother. Handwritten notes on everyone who will be voting on whether or not you're the next CEO, and suggestions on how to win them over."

He pressed his palm over the thick binder to hold it

against his chest and glanced down at it. "Hasn't she heard of email? The cloud?"

"*You* try telling her that," Violet said, smiling, then did a double take when she glanced behind him. He had female company all right, but not the kind she'd been fearing.

Violet pointed. "Is that my dog?"

Coco looked tiny and immensely happy on the center cushion of the sofa. Her little tail wagged furiously, but instead of jumping up to greet her mom, she rested her snout between tiny paws, looking up with beseeching eyes, as though to say *don't be mad*.

"Toto and I have been bonding," he said, moving aside in silent invitation.

Violet stepped inside, and Coco hopped off the couch and raced over in greeting.

"I distinctly remember dropping you off at your grandma Edith's house this afternoon when I picked up the binder," Violet told the dog, scooping her up and mock-glaring into her sweet little face.

"Edith had a last-minute invitation to some fussy art exhibit she couldn't resist, and Alvin . . . well, now I forget," Cain said. "Something to do with a rash and milk baths. I didn't ask for more details than that."

"So he called *you*?" Violet asked.

"Nope, I just happened to be there at the time, dropping something off. Your dog's a flirt and wouldn't leave me alone, so . . . here we are."

Violet kissed Coco's head, then set her down so she could dart back to the couch and claim her spot. "I could have sworn I put her in a little plaid sweater. What happened to it?"

"Hmm. Must have gotten lost."

"Uh-huh." Violet crossed her arms. "Wait. If you were over at Edith's house, why did she beg me to bring this binder over to you? She said it was urgent."

He tossed the binder onto the counter. "Come on, Duchess. You know this one. Because she's a meddling old busybody trying to push us together. Drink?"

Huh. Apparently Violet wasn't the only one who'd been on the receiving end of Edith's unsubtle matchmaking. She itched to ask him what Edith may have said, but instead she didn't want to risk upsetting the unusual truce between them. "Please. Wine, if you've got it."

"Prepare to be impressed. I have wine *and* wineglasses."

"You bought wineglasses?" she asked skeptically.

"Well, my trough was too big to ship to New York. And no. Adam had about two thousand fancy glasses. Brought a few with me, sold the rest."

"And the furniture?" she asked, accepting the glass and gesturing around at the furnished home. "You move fast."

"Kim hooked me up with some company that takes care of everything. You pick a package, and they bring you a couch, bed, lamps, that ugly brown rug."

"It's marigold. I sort of like it."

Cain shrugged, then hoisted himself onto the counter, sipping his beer as he studied her.

"Did they not have barstools in your package deal?" Violet asked.

"They were out of stock, getting delivered next week." Then he surprised her, by patting the counter beside him in invitation. And maybe in a bit of challenge.

Violet Townsend did *not* sit on counters, and Cain knew it.

She couldn't even fathom her grandmother's expression at the thought, or Edith's. Or Keith's. Or even Ashley's.

She handed Cain her glass of wine, and before she could rethink it, planted both palms on the counter and hauled herself up beside him, settling beside him and letting her legs dangle above the floor, her butt on cold marble. It felt both improper, and exactly right.

Cain handed her the wineglass back. "There's something I've been meaning to ask you," he said.

"Is it going to be rude?"

"You'll probably think so. You think everything is rude. But on a scale of one to ten, how comfortable are those shoes?" Cain asked, nodding down at her Jimmy Choos.

Violet followed his gaze to her ankle boots, blue suede with four-inch heels. She considered the question. "Is ten the most comfortable?"

He nodded. "Ten is slippers, one is wrapping your feet in barbed wire."

"Four," she said, then amended it. "No, three."

"Thought so. Take them off. I don't allow anything under a five in my home."

She looked down at his shoes, a little surprised to realize they were the loafers she'd picked out for him and not his usual scuffed boots or sneakers. "How comfortable are *yours?*"

"Six."

"That's all? They look more comfortable than anything I own."

"I'm sure they are, but I miss my boots."

Before she could protest, the toe of Cain's loafer hooked nimbly on the heel of her bootie and kicked it off.

Her mouth dropped open as the several-hundred-dollar shoe dropped indelicately to the hardwood floor. "You did not just."

"I did just." His foot tried with her other boot, but she laughingly pulled her leg out of reach. "I'll do it."

Lifting her leg, she eased the shoe off, though she hesitated before dropping it to the floor.

"Drop it, Duchess," he commanded. "Live on the edge."

"I don't know that dropping my shoe a couple feet counts as *extreme living.*"

"For you? It counts."

"What do you mean, *for me?*" she asked, looking over at him.

Violet expected him to be mocking, or at the very least

amused, but instead Cain's expression seemed almost . . . gentle. Encouraging.

She dropped the shoe, then held up her hand dramatically, showing it was empty. *Happy now?*

"So," she said, swinging her legs, enjoying the freedom of it. "Is this how Cain Stone spends Saturday nights?"

"Sometimes."

"I didn't expect you to be alone," she said.

He gestured toward the dog on the couch. "I'm not. I've got a hot piece of tail right there."

"That's not what I meant."

"I know," he said simply. "You eat?"

"I had a late lunch."

"I was going to order Italian. Want some?"

"I just came to drop off the binder, not to stay for dinner," she said.

"Noted." He reached out and flipped open the binder to a random page. "Where do you want to start?"

She glanced at the faded lined paper with Edith's neat but tiny old-fashioned cursive handwriting, where a photograph of one of the board members wearing a plastic expression and a boring tie smiled blandly back at her.

She let out a little groan of misery at the thought of reviewing it, and Cain snapped the binder shut again. "Thought so," he said.

"Wi-Fi and cable's hooked up," Cain said, apropos of nothing.

She blinked. "Congratulations?"

"How do you feel about Netflix?"

She considered. "I feel that beyond *Gossip Girl* reruns, I haven't put it to much use."

His hand closed over her knee, and he hopped off the counter. He held out a palm. "C'mon."

"Come on what?"

Their gazes locked for a moment, then Coco let out an excited bark from the couch, her little head poking around the edge, as though to say *get over here where it's comfortable!*

Cain removed his proffered palm, but before Violet could register regret that she'd missed the chance to touch him, his hands went to her waist, lifting her easily and setting her on the ground.

Instinctively, her hands went to his upper arms to steady herself as stockinged feet hit hardwood floor. She tilted her head to look up at him, finding him even taller than usual without her typical heels to mitigate their height difference.

She felt very small and soft. He seemed very tall and hard.

Female. Male.

Right.

Cain stepped back quickly, releasing her as though she'd burned him, before nodding jerkily in the direction of the TV. "Pick something. I veto subtitles and British accents. I'll get you more wine."

She wandered toward the table, looking for the remote. "Okay, then I get to veto gore."

"Deal. I also veto anything with kissing."

She gasped in horror as she picked the remote up off the coffee table and turned toward the enormous flatscreen. "Kissing's the best part of any film."

"Nope." He refilled her glass and got himself another beer. "Not the best part of movies, not the best part of real life either."

"What is the best part?"

"Fight scenes and sex."

"Of movies? Or real life?"

"Both."

She thought about this, then shook her head. "But sex is better with kissing," she argued, both surprised and delighted to hear herself even having this conversation. It was fun being around Cain when he didn't have his walls up. Playful, even.

"Maybe you've been having sex with the wrong dudes," he said, coming over and handing her the wineglass.

"Maybe you've been kissing the wrong women," Violet countered.

His eyes narrowed briefly, then he clinked the neck of his beer bottle to her glass in a silent toast and plopped down onto the couch. "Maybe I have."

The air between them seemed electric, but neither of

them mentioned their kiss the other night. Nor did Cain initiate a repeat.

Violet tried really hard to be glad about that fact.

Violet woke up with an uncomfortable crick in her neck and an instant awareness that she wasn't in her bedroom. There were no silk sheets. No soft down blanket. She was wearing a dress instead of her usual nightgown, and . . .

There was a man beneath her head, a dog curled up in her lap.

She went still at the realization, instinctively not wanting to wake either of them until she got her bearings.

She felt the steady thud of his heartbeat beneath her palm, felt the comforting softness of the worn fabric of a T-shirt against her cheek.

Cain.

The sleep fog cleared, and the night's events came back to her. Coming here and finding her dog. The wine. The action movie binge. The glut of pasta. She'd had a little wine, he'd had a few beers, and they'd simply . . . hung out.

Talked when they'd felt like it. Sat in silence when they'd felt like it. She'd remembered getting drowsy, feeling more content than she had in years . . .

She'd fallen asleep. On a strange man's couch.

Except he wasn't strange, he was becoming . . . important.

The TV was off now, the room silent and still, and Violet felt like she could hear every heartbeat, his and hers.

Coco shifted sleepily in her lap, and Violet stroked a hand over the dog's back, but otherwise didn't move. Not yet. Cain's arm had come around Violet in his sleep, his hand resting heavily on her waist, as though he'd reached for her instinctively and then held her close.

It was all too easy to picture waking up like this every morning.

Jarred by the realization, she eased away from Cain, carefully lifting his arm so she could slip from beneath it. Coco gave her a protesting, indignant look and stood, shifting from Violet's lap to Cain's, where she curled up once more.

Cain didn't awake fully, but must have sensed Coco's presence, because the hand that had been holding Violet close moved to settle protectively over the little dog. Violet nearly whimpered at the cuteness.

Standing, she padded carefully over the wood floor on stockinged feet. Violet picked up her shoes and pulled her phone out of her purse to check the time.

4:45 a.m. Much closer to the time she usually got up than the time she generally went to bed. Her alarm would be going off at 6:00.

Violet carried her shoes to the door, planning to put them on once outside his apartment, so the click of her high heels wouldn't wake him up.

She turned back to look at Cain and Coco, wishing the man had a throw blanket she could cover him with when she left. Violet made a mental note to get him one.

His features were softer when he slept. Most people's features were, she supposed, but it was more pronounced with someone as guarded and masculine as Cain. With his long, curly lashes resting along his cheeks, hiding the usual harsh cynicism in his eyes, Cain seemed almost angelic, albeit of the Lucifer variety.

His hair had come loose from its tie, with strands framing his strong jawline, brushing his shoulders. Her gaze shifted again, this time to his beard. Not for the first time, she wondered how it felt. Prickly? Scratchy? Smooth?

Violet bit her lip as she realized this might be her only chance to find out. It would be horribly intrusive, touching someone as they slept without their knowing, and yet . . .

She took a deep breath and walked back to him. She slowly reached out, her hand coming closer and closer to his face until the pads of her fingers lightly touched his cheek.

She froze, waiting to see if he'd wake, but he didn't stir. Violet moved her hand softly, finding the texture of his beard was different than she'd expected. It was soft, almost silky when she slid her fingers down toward his jaw but turned prickly when she dragged them lightly upward against the direction of hair growth.

Research completed, Violet ordered herself to pick up her dog and leave. Instead, she stayed where she was, her hand on his face in a light caress.

Long, strong fingers closed around her wrist, and Violet gasped, her breath coming out on a whoosh.

Her gaze flew to Cain's. He blinked twice, his brown eyes still soft with sleep. She waited for his anger to register, even as her brain scrambled for a plausible explanation as to why she was touching his face in his sleep, when he was most vulnerable, like a total weirdo.

The anger never came, though. Instead, he remained perfectly still, her wrist still locked in his grip, her hand cupping his cheek. She wanted to know what he was thinking. Wanted to know whatever went on behind those guarded, dark eyes of his. Wanted to know *him*.

"You need help getting home?" he asked into her hand, his voice rough with sleep.

"No." It came out as a whisper, and she tried again. "No, there are plenty of cabs right outside your place. I'll be fine."

He started to stir as though to come with her, but she shook her head quickly. "No. I'm fine. Really."

Cain hesitated, then nodded. "Text me when you get in the cab. And again when you get home."

She smiled a little at the protective note in his voice. Sleepy Cain, with his guard down, was . . . compelling. "I will."

She slowly pulled her hand away from his face, and his fingers tightened reflexively before releasing her.

Scooping up her dog, Violet went to the door and slipped her shoes on before picking up her jacket and purse. It was too small to carry Coco, so she kept the sleeping pup carefully against her stomach, lifting her other hand to wave goodbye to Cain.

She couldn't think of a single thing to say. *Thank you? Good night? Good morning?*

Do you feel what I feel?

She asked none of this, because the sleepiness was gone from his gaze, replaced by his usual guarded wariness.

Violet slipped out the front door, closing it with a quiet click.

The early morning was quiet, the bars having closed an hour ago and even the most die-hard partiers at home in their beds. Or someone else's.

As expected, she had no problem hailing a cab right outside Cain's building. She opened the door, pausing for a moment, before looking up at his apartment.

She couldn't be sure in the darkness, but she thought she saw the shadow of a man watching her from the fourth-floor windows.

Violet got into the cab, and after giving the driver her address, pulled out her phone to text Cain as Coco settled into a tight puppy ball on her lap. In cab.

His response was immediate. I know.

Violet smiled. So he *had* been watching her. Creeper.

Says the woman who was watching me sleep.

She smiled wider, surprised to find that she was completely unembarrassed. I confess, I'd been wondering about the texture of your beard.

And?

And now I know.

She let out a little laugh at her own coy response, then covered her mouth in surprise at the sound. Who *was* this woman flirting over texts?

Huh.

She frowned at his cryptic response. Damn. He was better at the game than she was. She was dying to know what he was thinking.

Violet didn't reply until she got home, texting Cain once again when she'd let herself into the apartment that she was home safe.

Good. Good night Duchess.

Good night. Or good morning.

It's a good something.

Violet smiled as she went into her bedroom. It was, indeed, a good something.

She just wasn't entirely sure what.

Sixteen

Violet nodded in thanks as the hostess pointed out her party, then made her way through the swanky downtown steakhouse toward the group.

At noon on a Monday, every table was filled with the power-lunch set, and on the surface, Violet was completely in her element. She knew how to dress, how to walk, how to school her features into an expression that was friendly but not *too* friendly. All of which created the persona of "you can come talk to me, but don't *actually* come talk to me."

Today, however, something was off. She was adorned in her usual uniform. A bouncy, shiny blowout, an understated but flattering maroon sheath dress with matching pumps, a handbag that was atrociously expensive.

But instead of feeling like armor, today it felt like a costume.

Not because of the clothes themselves, but because the woman beneath them no longer felt placid and resigned. She felt invigorated and excited about life, on the verge of *something*, even though she hadn't quite figured out what.

Violet did know, however, that she was not excited to be *here*, in this restaurant, on this day, with these people. It certainly wasn't the first time Edith had invited Violet to lunch on a weekday, but this time the invitation had felt tense and loaded, though the older woman hadn't provided Violet any clues on context.

Concern had her footsteps slowing ever so slightly as she registered the faces sitting around the table. She'd figured on Edith, of course. And she'd known that Rhodes' board members Jocelyn Stevens and Dan Bogan would be joining as well.

But one man was unexpectedly absent: Cain.

Another man was even more unexpectedly present:

Keith.

Dan and Keith both stood as Violet approached, their polite, chivalrous manners as ingrained in them as Violet's fake smile was in her.

Violet was apprehensive as she caught Keith's eye, searching for any sign that he resented her for their recent breakup. He merely smiled warmly and pulled out her chair the way he had hundreds of times in the past.

She supposed she should be relieved that he was being so decent about the breakup, making it clear that there was no bad blood between them. But she couldn't help but wonder if there shouldn't be at least a touch of awkwardness?

What did it say about their relationship that its demise didn't cause even the *slightest* ripple?

"Violet, it's so wonderful to see you again," Jocelyn was saying. "We really appreciate you taking the time to join us today."

"Of course, my pleasure," Violet lied easily, sipping her ice water and glancing subtly at Edith for some clue as to what was going on. But the other woman didn't meet her eye, and Violet was alarmed to see how frail and tired Edith looked.

Conversation moved almost immediately toward the typical rounds of small talk: Weather, weekend recaps, and everyone's plans for the upcoming Oscars.

Violet joined in, said all the right things, even as her irritation and impatience with the situation notched upward with every new mundane topic that circled the table.

Get to the point, she wanted to scream, even as she kept her expression carefully pleasant.

Finally, as soup and salads were served, Dan Bogan cut through the crap.

Violet didn't know him well. Not because she hadn't met him dozens of times over the years, but because she wasn't sure there was much to know. He was a senior board member, and had been a close friend of Edith's late husband. Dan was friendly with Edith as well, but she'd always sensed the friendship was more one of convenience and shared interests than genuine affection.

Violet had never particularly liked or disliked the man. But she was disliking him now.

"So, Violet," Dan said with a placid smile. "First, I think I speak for all of us when I say you've done a remarkable job with Cain."

Violet forced a smile, but the "compliment" bothered her. Cain wasn't a home renovation or a work assignment. He was a human being.

"He's barely *recognizable* from just a few weeks ago," Jocelyn added with a cheerful smile. "In demeanor, anyway. Much more polished."

Violet heard the caveat loud and clear. "In demeanor?"

Joycelyn glanced at Edith, who remained stoically silent as she sipped her iced tea.

"Let me just preface this all by saying everyone here wants to see Cain take the company reins," Keith interjected.

Violet gave him a blatantly challenging look. "Everyone?"

His eyes narrowed briefly, but his smile never dropped. "Yes, Vi. Everyone. But the thing is . . ."

The table fell silent for a moment as everyone danced around whatever they were all thinking but nobody wanted to be the one to say it aloud.

Finally, it was Edith who gathered her gumption and got to the point.

"They think he looks like a lumberjack," Edith said bluntly.

Jocelyn let out a dismayed noise.

"Edith," Dan said. "That isn't what we said."

"But it's what you meant, Dan," Edith said with a chilly smile. "You sent me a four-paragraph email about his *hair*."

"We just think," Jocelyn said, turning to Violet, "that with the vote a week and a half away, we need to lock this thing up all the way. During Cain's round of interviews, it would help if he—"

"What interviews?" Violet asked, glancing around the table.

She'd known that *everything* Cain had been put through these past few weeks was an interview of sorts, but she hadn't realized there'd be formal interviews.

"It's a new addition to the process," Dan said smoothly. "Every board member will get a chance to question Cain personally to see if he's the right fit."

"I see. And whose idea was this *new addition*?" she asked.

"It's not an unreasonable request, Vi," Keith said. "We're talking about putting the man at the helm of a billion-dollar company. It's only fair that the board members feel as comfortable as they can be before handing over the reins."

"And Cain's hair will make a difference?"

"Perceptions are important. You know that as well as we do, otherwise you wouldn't have agreed to Edith's request in the first place."

She did know. She just hated it.

Violet looked around the table. "What is it exactly you want me to do? Pin him down, wielding a razor?"

"We just thought you might *suggest* a new look. These sorts of things are always better coming from a beautiful woman."

Dan smiled, but for the first time in her life, Violet didn't automatically smile back for the sole purpose of making him feel comfortable.

He *should* be uncomfortable. He should be ashamed.

"I see," Violet said after a pregnant silence. "Is there anything else I should have Cain prepare for? Will there be a hoop to jump through? A ball for him to balance on his nose?"

Violet looked at Edith. "Is this what you want? Your legacy to be determined based on a *haircut*?"

"What I want has little bearing on reality," Edith said in a defeated tone.

Dan and Joycelyn both had the decency to look awkward as they became suddenly interested in their meals, but Keith's attention was entirely on Violet.

"What's changed?" Keith asked Violet.

She glared at him defiantly. "What do you mean?"

"How is what we're suggesting any different from what you agreed to? You've spent the past few weeks introducing him to cashmere, and keeping his elbows off the table, and teaching him how to appreciate art, and erasing *ain't*s from his vernacular. All we're asking now is more of the same."

"You're right. It's not all that different," she agreed.

Keith glanced at Jocelyn and Dan in surprise.

"What's changed isn't the nature of the request, so much as my willingness to acquiesce to it," Violet said. "Helping him adjust to a new city and new job responsibilities is one thing, but I regret any part I've had in making that man think his worth is measured in the length of his hair or whether he prefers boots to loafers."

Violet set her napkin on the table beside the bowl of untouched lobster bisque. "Cain deserves to be measured on his merit, and his merit alone. I'll mention the haircut to him, because it should be his choice if he wants to play your game. But if he asks my opinion, I'll give it to him plainly. I think he should tell the whole board to go screw itself." She stood. "Now if you'll excuse me, I seem to have lost my appetite."

Seventeen

⁓

You actually said that?" Ashley asked with a delighted laugh. "Damn, I wish I could have seen it."

"I keep waiting to feel ashamed or guilty about it," Violet said, smiling herself. "But I'd repeat my entire speech all over again if given the chance. They were *horrid*."

"Do you think Cain'll go through with it? The cut, the shave, the whole deal?"

"I don't know," Violet said truthfully. "I'll do as promised and mention it to him, because I believe he deserves to have all the information, and make his own decisions. But if I had to guess, he's going to be pissed. Not so much at the suggestion of a haircut and shave—no huge surprise there—but because they met with me behind his back, discussing him as though he's a mannequin to be positioned and placed and styled at their will."

"Well, if he does decide to do it, I'm glad I'm meeting him now before he goes through with it," Ashley said.

She looped her arm through Violet's as they made their way down Fifth Avenue, then gave a contented sigh. "Is there any better feeling than playing hooky on a weekday?"

Ashley's boss was out of town at a conference, and they'd taken advantage of the extra flexibility in her schedule to meet for a long, late lunch of Cobb salad, profiteroles, and sparkling lemonade before Violet's appointment to meet Cain at the tailor's to see how the rush job on the gala tuxedo had turned out.

"You'd know better than me," Violet said to Ashley, distracted for a moment by a particularly cute Tiffany window display. "I'm guessing playing hooky feels different with a paying job."

"Something you would be more familiar with if you quit being so stubborn," Ashley said with the gentle chiding of a good friend. "Edith has offered to pay you for years for all the random crap you do for her. The party planning. The errands. Buying the perfect gifts for her employees."

"It would feel weird taking Edith's money," Violet replied. "I don't need it. And I'm happy to help her out."

Ashley said nothing, and Violet knew her friend's silence was a deliberate decision to steer them clear of an old argument. Violet's volunteer status as Edith's assistant wasn't something that they saw eye to eye on.

Violet could see her friend's point, in theory, but she also had never had the slightest interest in becoming an official Rhodes employee. She'd always thought it was because she didn't need the money, and working for Edith "for free" felt like the least she could do to help out a woman who'd taken her in.

Now, however, she was wondering if there wasn't another reason she'd been resistant to the idea of a steady paycheck:

She didn't want to do it forever. She wasn't sure she wanted to do it at all. Violet wondered if some part of her was resisting this path, demanding that she search harder for what she wanted from her life.

Violet was finally searching. She just hadn't found any answers.

"Does Cain know I'm tagging along today?" Ashley asked curiously.

"No, and I hear that excited tone, but, Ash, I'd temper your expectations a bit," Violet warned. "Cain's not exactly the charming, easy-to-talk-to type you're used to."

"Even better. I love rooting for an underdog."

"Cain Stone is no underdog," Violet said. "More . . . dark horse."

"Damn, that's sexy," Ashley said, then stopped and set her hand on Violet's shoulder, adjusting the heel of her stiletto. "Hold up. New shoes, and incoming blister alert. How close are we?"

"Two more blocks. It's the same tailor Keith uses."

Ashley's professionally shaped eyebrows lifted. "*Interest-*

ing. And how does Keith feel about the fact that you're using his tailor to dress up the enemy?"

Violet shrugged. "What he won't know won't hurt him. Plus, we broke up."

"Well, *I* can tell you what he'll think if he finds out," Ashley said with confidence as they resumed walking. "He'd hate it. They're already two dogs after the same bone. Bad news to send them to the same groomer."

Violet laughed at the metaphor. "I'm not sure how Edith would feel about the CEO position of her beloved company being compared to a bone."

"Oh, sweetie." Ashley smiled indulgently. "The *job's* not the bone. You are."

Violet rolled her eyes, nodding for Ashley to turn onto Fifty-Sixth. "Right here."

Violet had been expecting to have to wait for Cain. He'd agreed—reluctantly—to meet her at the tailor's at three, and she and Ashley were a bit early.

So was Cain. His eyes found hers, and she remembered that the last time she'd seen him, she'd woken up curled against his chest, feeling safe, and warm, and . . . *home*.

He was standing at the side of the building, leaning into a service door, booted foot propped up against it. Not looking at his phone, not doing anything besides watching them approach, with his trademark unreadable glower.

He lowered his boot to the ground and straightened, and Violet heard Ashley's feminine purr of approval. Cain was wearing the gray wool coat they'd bought together, as well as a light gray sweater overtop a collared shirt. The jeans, Violet realized, were the old ones he'd brought with him, and the boots definitely hadn't been purchased in New York.

The combination of Manhattan polish and outsider defiance was intensely attractive.

Ashley extended her hand with a warm smile. "You must be Cain."

When Cain's usual guarded expression relaxed immediately as he shook her friend's hand, Violet felt a little stab of envy that she'd never inspired the same instant ease in people.

Violet thought she'd stopped envying Ashley's sunny charisma years ago, but the smile Cain gave Ashley was easier, and more friendly within seconds of meeting, than any he'd given Violet in the month they'd known each other.

Then again, perhaps she shouldn't be surprised. Violet's reserved presence had always been the kind that made men check to see that their tie knot was perfectly straight, to adjust their shirt cuffs just so. Ashley was the type of woman who caused men to *loosen* their tie, to roll up their sleeves.

Violet had little doubt which type of woman Cain gravitated toward.

Ashley glanced at her watch. "I hate to bail on a free fashion show, and I love a man in a tux, but I'll have to wait until the Heart Ball to see you all pretty," she said, batting her eyelashes playfully at Cain. "I have to at least *pretend* I did a bit of work this afternoon before my wretched co-worker tattles to my boss about my too-long lunch."

"I'll take pictures," Violet volunteered, waggling her phone.

"Not if you want that phone to stay in one piece you won't," Cain said. "And by the way, you *do* realize I can manage to try on a penguin suit without your presence."

"Uh-huh." She gave him an arch look. "So you *didn't* call Zeke and tell him you didn't need the tux after all?"

He didn't look even remotely guilty. "Actually, my exact words were I wasn't going to spend hundreds of dollars on a penguin suit I'll wear once in a decade."

"I don't know what's cuter, that you think it'll only be hundreds of dollars, or that you'll only wear it once a decade." Ashley patted his bicep good-naturedly, then blew a kiss to Violet before departing with a cheerful wave.

Inside the shop, as they waited for his tux to be brought out front, Cain picked up a business card off the reception desk. He scraped the pad of his thumb over the corner, as though testing the paper quality.

"I thought we were going to have lunch," he said abruptly, a bit curt. "You were going to bore my head off with an explanation of how to navigate a wine list, remember?"

She froze in confusion. "When, today? No, we weren't. I've had plans with Ashley for days."

He shook his head. "Not today. Monday."

Monday. The day she'd met with Edith, Keith, Dan, and Jocelyn.

"Something came up." She kept her voice light.

"Right. And how *was* the duke? Trying to get you back?"

"How did you know I had lunch with—" Violet broke off, realizing the obviousness of the answer. Keith had obviously let it slip that they'd had lunch together. And she was betting not by accident.

Maybe Ashley was right. Maybe she *was* the bone.

"Sorry about the delay!" Zeke interrupted the impending argument, coming out from the back room, the tux draped over his arm. "My wife called, and since she's eight months pregnant, I live in a pretty much constant state of agitation that every call is going to be *the* call."

"Oh! Congratulations! *Was* it the baby call?" Violet asked. "If you need to reschedule . . ."

"No, no," Zeke said with a reassuring smile. "Just a gentle wifely reminder that I promised to let out her favorite dress in time for a party this weekend." He gestured around his belly, miming a bump.

"Come with me, Mr. Stone," Zeke said, beckoning Cain forward. "Violet, sweetheart, make yourself comfortable over there with the magazines."

Violet did as instructed, but though she opened the latest issue of *Vogue*, she couldn't focus. She didn't *want* to read about fascinators having a moment on the runway. She wanted a damn manual on Cain Stone, and his mercurial moods, and . . .

Her muddled thoughts vanished when the dressing room curtain was jerked open and Cain stepped into view.

Violet stared and mentally uttered a phrase right out of his playbook. *Holy shit.*

Cain in jeans and a T-shirt had a sort of raw magnetism. In a suit, he'd been all sexy professional. Cain in a tux, though, amplified that by a hundred. Not because he looked like Keith or any of the other businessmen in Violet's acquaintance, but because he didn't.

There was a large, floor-length mirror along one side of the shop, but Cain didn't so much as glance at it. Instead, he fixed his gaze on Violet, his dark eyes glowering. He lifted a shoulder, irritated. *Well? Happy now?*

Violet swallowed. "You look . . . nice."

Zeke laughed and put a hand over his heart. "*Nice?* Just stab me; it would hurt less."

"Better than nice," she amended as she stood. "Men's fashion isn't really my expertise, but even I can see . . ." She walked toward Cain, then motioned for him to spin, mostly to annoy him.

He stayed perfectly still, mostly to annoy *her.*

"Do I pass muster?" he snapped when she came full circle back in front of him.

She stepped up to him, needlessly adjusting the lapel. "You'll do."

It was hard to remember that the tailor who had sewn the dozens of suits in Keith's closet had also sewn this one. She'd seen Keith in a tux that looked just like this one, but he didn't wear it this way.

Cain's shoulders seemed extra broad, his waist extra narrow, his legs extra long. He looked like a perfect Wall Street specimen, except . . .

"Where's your hair band?" she asked.

He lifted his hand, raked his fingers through his long hair. "Must have come out while I was changing."

Violet could have gone to look for it. Or gotten one of the bands she knew she had somewhere in her purse. But she didn't.

With his black hair falling over the collar of his shirt, his short beard dark against the crisp white, he looked . . . good.

It was also exactly the opening she needed.

Violet glanced at the tailor. "Zeke, can we have a minute?"

He nodded. "I'll be in the back. Holler if you need me."

Violet waited until he was gone, then faced Cain. "I need to talk to you about something."

He fussed with the bow tie irritably. "What?"

She took a deep breath. "That lunch on Monday with Keith, it wasn't personal, and it wasn't just the two of us. Edith was there. Dan and Jocelyn as well."

"And?"

He was becoming more impatient by the moment, so Violet spit it out bluntly.

"The board wants me to talk you into cutting your hair."

Violet expected his anger, but the flash of hurt on his face caught her right in the throat. He shut it down quickly, resuming a mask of surly indifference. "Well, at least now I know what the other night was about."

"I don't follow," she said, genuinely confused.

"At my place. The whole flirty, watch Netflix and eat pasta routine—what was that, buttering me up for the final stage of my transformation into Boy Barbie? Sorry, babe, but you're going to have to put out a hell of a lot more than a movie night." He gave her a deliberately insulting once-over.

It was Violet's turn to be angry. And hurt. "First of all, that night was *your* idea," she said, gratified when his jaw tensed in silent acquiescence to the point. "Second of all, I never said I thought you should cut your hair. I just said *they* do."

He snorted. "Please. You've practically been panting to turn me into a mannequin."

"I was," Violet admitted. "At the start. Not anymore."

"Ah," he said coldly. "So then you've finally decided. It's the bad boy that gets your juices flowing."

Violet studied him for a long moment, waited for her temper to get under control, then nodded slowly. "Okay, Cain. Okay. Here's what I told them." She stepped closer, enjoying the way his gaze went wary. "I told them that I'd pass along their message. Then I told them to go screw themselves."

His face betrayed nothing.

Violet stepped even closer. "And you know what? You were dead-on about me. I *do* change my behavior based on who I am with. I *have* spent too much of my life trying to be what other people want me to be. But you know, Cain? I'd rather try and fail than live like you."

His eyes narrowed, daring her to continue, and she did.

"You're the oldest cliché in the book: you reject everyone before they can reject you." She gave him a sad look. "Congratulations. It's working like a charm."

He said nothing, and Violet finally gave up, shaking her head and picking up her purse. Her smile was bittersweet. On the personal growth front, she knew she'd just taken a step forward: speaking her mind instead of placating.

So why didn't she feel better?

Text Exchange between Ashley and Violet

Ashley: Okay, you're officially the worst best friend ever. You didn't tell me that he looked like THAT.

Violet: You looked up his picture! You knew he was good-looking.

Ashley: The appeal of men like Cain can't be captured in pictures. I'm still all hot and bothered, and it's been an hour since I met him.

Violet: Well, he's all yours if you want him. I'm done.

Eighteen

ow long do we have to stay?" Violet asked Ashley grumpily as she shrugged off her coat.

"That's usually my line," Ashley said. She took Violet's coat and tossed it, and her own, onto the "coat pile" chair in Jenny and Mike Kaling's entryway. "You're the one who tells *me* we have to at least make an appearance."

"I know," Violet said wearily, surreptitiously adjusting the strapless bra that was digging into her rib cage. "Let's do this."

"Forty-five minutes, tops," Ashley said as they made their way to the buzzing kitchen, where the guests had congregated. "Long enough to have a drink, tell Mike happy birthday, and then Irish goodbye—uh-oh."

Violet glanced at her friend. "What's wrong?"

"You may have been doing a little too good of a job

introducing Cain around town." She nodded across the kitchen, and Violet glanced over her shoulder.

Her stomach sank.

Cain was here.

She should have been prepared. She'd introduced him to Jenny and Mike last week, and they'd made a point to invite him to the party. But Violet hadn't expected him to actually come.

She definitely hadn't expected him to come *with* someone.

Nor had she been prepared for how much it would hurt. It's not as though they were together. They had no understanding. One angry kiss and a movie night hardly made up for the dozens of far less pleasant interactions between them, the most recent fight at the tailor's the freshest.

Not fifteen minutes ago, she'd declared to Ashley in the taxi that she was done trying to figure him out, done trying to win over a man who thought the worst of her.

Cain could not have made it plainer that the only thing he wanted from her was distance, and she was more than happy to give it to him.

And yet here they were in the same room, and seeing him laughing with another woman was . . . fine! Just fine.

She just wanted to barf, was all.

"Ugh, Alison Grape. I've never liked her," Ashley said in disgust as the gorgeous blonde in a tight dress touched Cain's arm, then whispered something in his ear when he bent down to her.

Violet didn't much like Alison either, though she couldn't have really said why. They had several mutual friends and frequently found themselves at the same bachelorette party or baby shower. They were perfectly friendly to each other, but for some reason had never clicked or made any effort to hang out when not required to by mutual friends.

Alison and Cain, on the other hand, seemed to be clicking just fine.

His head tilted back as he laughed long and loud at something Alison said, and Violet quickly turned her head away. He *never* laughed with her.

"Oh, *God*," Ashley said with agonized feeling as she poured them each a glass of wine. She thrust one at Violet. "Here, drink this. All of it, quick. Quick."

"Why?"

"Because this bad party's about to get even worse."

Worse? Impossible.

"Good to see you too, Ash," came a bemused male voice.

Violet turned, seeing that Ashley had been very correct: the party *could* get worse. "Hello, Keith."

He held her gaze for a moment, then glanced at Ashley. "Can we have a minute?"

"Nope." Ashley sipped her wine and stayed stubbornly put.

"Ash," Violet said softly.

Her friend huffed. "Okay, two minutes. And only because I have to pee. Make yourself useful and hold this,"

Ashley said, handing Keith her wineglass. "Do not upset my best friend, or—" She mimed a throat-slashing gesture.

"She's the one who dumped me," Keith pointed out.

Ashley ignored this, using her two fingers to point to her eyes, then Keith. *I'm watching you.*

"You'd better hope she never switches allegiances," Keith said in amusement as Ashley headed for the bathroom line.

"She won't," Violet said, sneaking another nonchalant glance over at Cain. If he'd noticed her arrival, he didn't show it. Though she supposed it would have been hard for him to notice much of anything given that all of his attention was on Alison's perky cleavage.

"You look incredible," Keith said, and Violet forced her attention back to him.

"Thanks."

His blue eyes searched hers. "I miss you, Vi."

She shifted uncomfortably. "Keith . . ."

"No, hear me out. Please," he added, sounding nothing like his usual strident, self-absorbed self. "It's been killing me not to call or text you. I've even come by your building a few times, but I forced myself to leave before knocking on the door. I wanted to give you space."

Warning bells sounded in the back of her head at the pleading, stubborn look on his face. She hoped Ashley made that pee *fast.*

"I appreciate that, Keith, but it's not so much that I needed space, but more that—"

"I care about you, Violet," he interrupted, his expression earnest now. "I didn't realize how much until you weren't there, and I know that's rotten of me. But I need you to know: I'll wait. If you change your mind, if you give me another chance—I'll be here. I'll always be here for you, no matter what."

Violet swallowed, uncomfortably aware of how close his words confirmed Edith's from the other day. Keith *was* the guy who would be there. Imperfectly, perhaps, but he'd still be there.

The very opposite of what Cain Stone offered, which was nothing.

She glanced over to see him talking to Jenny and Mike, Alison still glued to his side.

All of a sudden, it felt like too much. Cain was doing exactly what she'd been trying to help him do. Assimilate into her world.

So why did she feel like the one on the outside?

And for the first time in her adult life, Violet couldn't muster the motivation to do and say the right thing, to stand here enduring a tepid speech from Keith, when she wanted to be anywhere else.

Violet didn't care that it was rude, didn't care that there were witnesses.

She just wanted to be anywhere but here, with this man, in this room . . .

"I—excuse me. I need some air," Violet said, pushing past

Keith and heading out to the patio. It was frigid outside, but she knew from past parties that the Kalings had heaters installed on the balcony.

The patio was less crowded than the kitchen, but she wasn't alone either. She moved in the direction of a trio of twenty-somethings, not because she knew them, but because they'd huddled beneath the heater.

The lone woman in the group smiled as Violet approached and shifted slightly to make room, before returning to her conversation. "Did you guys *see* him?" she asked her male companions. "I'd heard he had his own look, but I thought everyone was exaggerating."

"I was in a projections meeting with him last night," one of the men said in a boastful tone. "The guy didn't say a single word the entire time, just looked intently at everyone who spoke, like a dog trying desperately to understand what its owner is trying to tell it, but the poor thing's brain is too small."

They all laughed, and the other man chimed in. "You don't seriously think he's going to take over, do you? Just because he's the old lady's long-lost grandson? That's some soap opera bullshit."

Violet went still as the words registered. There was absolutely no chance they weren't talking about Edith and Cain.

"Oh, there's no way he'll get the job, but you can't blame the woman for trying," one of the gossipers said confidently. "If I were Edith Rhodes, I'd want my cake and eat it too. Go through the motions of letting the guy *think* she's trying to help him get the job so she has someone to visit her in the nursing home someday, but when push comes to shove, she'll do what's best for the business."

The twinges of resentment she felt at not ruffling feathers, of always doing the proper thing while talking to Keith blossomed to full-on rebellion. She may be mad as hell at Cain, and she too may have questioned Edith's determination to have Cain take over, but she wouldn't sit idly by and politely avoid confrontation while three strangers discussed people she cared about as though they were contestants on the latest reality TV show.

Violet stepped toward the group, knowing her eyes were flashing with her anger, and not really caring. "And what do you think *is* best for the business?"

Three pairs of startled eyes glanced her way, panicked at first, then turning to thinly veiled derisiveness when she was deemed a nobody.

"Sorry," the guy said, not sounding the least bit sorry. "Three-way conversation here." He gestured with his beer among the trio.

"Conversation?" Violet tilted her head with fake confusion. "Or petty gossip?"

"Um, no offense," the woman said with passive-aggressive friendliness. "But you don't even know who or what we're talking about."

"Don't I?" Violet asked with such icy confidence that

the younger woman blinked, her bravado replaced with nervousness.

"Take it from someone more familiar with the situation than you three underlings," Violet said. "The reason Edith is considering Cain Stone as CEO is because he has more brains, integrity, and civility in a single eyelash than the three of you have combined."

"What the—" The rest of the guy's sentence sputtered off into boozy anger.

"Are any of you Rhodes board members?" Violet asked rhetorically, since she knew all the key players at the company, and none of these brats qualified. "No? Nobody? Huh. Well, here's a last bit of advice. Enjoy the kids' table, because it's as far as any of you will ever get."

Violet had always wanted to pivot dramatically on her heel, and she did so now, delighted that she'd opted for a dress, which added a bit more flair to the gesture.

She started to walk away from the gaping trio and pulled up short when she saw a man leaning against the railing, a beer bottle swinging idly from his fingers, his expression blank.

He lifted the bottle to his lips and his eyebrows to her. "Quite the speech there, Duchess."

So. He'd heard.

"Shit," she muttered.

His mouth twisted in an almost-smile at her uncharacteristic profanity.

"I'm mad at you," she snapped a bit childishly, snatching his beer out of his hand and taking a gulp. Belying her words, she shifted to stand beside him rather than walking away. They both leaned against the railing, hip to hip, shoulder to shoulder, companionably watching the party, as though there weren't fireworks between them with every other encounter.

"Fair," Cain said.

Violet gave him a wary look. "So you acknowledge you were an ass at the tailor's?"

He gazed over at the recipients of Violet's stinging setdown, but she got the impression he wasn't really seeing them.

"Not just then," Cain said quietly.

"That doesn't sound like an apology."

He smiled slightly, reaching out to take his beer back. "Then perhaps you weren't listening properly."

Violet told herself to go back inside, to find Ashley. Even Keith would be safer. Her feet didn't move, as though the stupid appendages preferred staying out here with a man who aroused her anger to the tepid rounds of small talk that awaited her inside.

"Saw you talking to the duke," Cain said, interrupting her thoughts.

It was on the tip of Violet's tongue to tell him that it was absolutely none of his business, but something in his tone stopped her. Beneath the usual mockery, there was a touch of earnestness. Of . . . vulnerability?

"Saw you talking to Alison," she said in return.

Talking. Flirting . . .

Cain lifted a shoulder, and then shifted slightly, to study her profile. "You and the duke back together, or what? He looked like a lovesick swain."

Violet reached for his beer again without looking at him. "We are not back together."

"But he wants to be."

She made a noncommittal noise.

"He does, but you don't," Cain guessed.

Violet sipped the beer again, a little surprised how good it tasted. She'd never fancied herself a beer drinker, but she liked the way the slight effervescence rolled over her tongue, the way the bottle felt in her hands.

He didn't respond. Not that she expected him to. She was beginning to *know* the man. Understood that he—

"I don't know what I want," Violet said, peeling at the label on the bottle with her thumbnail.

Without warning, Cain slipped a hand behind her head and, pulling her face toward his, kissed her.

His lips boldly explored hers, firm and warm. The kiss seemed to say everything he wouldn't aloud, but it felt like a code that she couldn't *quite* crack.

Cain pulled back and straightened, releasing Violet as suddenly as he'd reached for her. He grinned shamelessly and reclaimed his beer bottle. "I don't care about Alice."

"Alison."

"Whatever."

She rolled her eyes. "I guess I shouldn't be surprised you don't know her name. I'm not even sure you know *mine*."

She'd never heard him call her anything but the gently mocking *Duchess*.

"I know it. Course I know it."

Violet didn't turn her head, just cut her gaze his way. "Are we going to talk about that kiss, or ignore it like we did the last one?"

He tipped the bottle up to his lips, smiling. But he said nothing.

Nineteen

"Oh, thank God you're here," Alvin said, already reaching to scoop Coco out of Violet's Chanel bag.

"I came as soon as I got your texts. What's the matter?" she asked, surreptitiously giving him a once-over and trying to figure out whether it was a perceived bacterial infection, a bruise he thought signaled cirrhosis, an itchy spot on his arm that he'd read was a symptom of a rare blood disease . . .

She was startled by the sound of loud, angry voices coming from the parlor.

"*That's* what's wrong," Alvin said.

"Oh dear," Violet said, feeling nonplussed. She hadn't heard yelling in Edith's house . . . ever. "Maybe I'll just go in and—"

The door flew open, and Cain stormed out. He halted when he saw Violet.

His hair was down around his shoulders, eyes blazing, shoulders hunched as though ready for a fight. Or perhaps already in the *middle* of a fight, Violet realized as Edith came to the doorway, looking plenty stormy herself.

Violet blinked. She'd never seen the older woman like this. Edith practically crackled with disapproval, all of her angry energy directed at her grandson.

"If you leave now, you'll undo all of our hard work," she said, her tone like a whip in its frustrated fury.

"I'm not leaving forever," he snapped back at her. "Just a few days. You and the company survived twenty-something years without me, I think you can spare me for three fucking days."

"The vote is in *one week*," Edith said. "This is crunch time. If you walk away, it'll show the board you're not prioritizing this. That you're still—"

"Still what?" Cain whirled around on his grandmother. "Still a piece of shit from the bayou? Still a slacker?"

Edith's nostrils flared. "We can't afford to let them see you as a quitter. Or someone who takes off on a whim."

"A *quitter*." Cain's hands landed on his hips. "What you mean is I can't quit *your* agenda. Because you have no issues with the fact that I turned my back on my real life in New Orleans. You didn't hesitate to ask me to walk away from *my* business, my friends, colleagues . . ."

"I'm sure people can load up trucks just fine without your careful supervision."

Violet winced. It was a horribly condescending thing to say. She knew it even before Cain's expression turned thunderous.

"You're right about one thing. My team is more than capable," he said. "But you're not the business-minded genius you think you are if you assume I'll leave them to deal with the Mardi Gras rush on their own while I sit in a fancy conference room drinking Italian espresso."

"Well then, you might as well kiss the company goodbye," Edith said. "Because sitting around in fancy conference rooms is what we *do*."

"Do it without me for three days. Three days is all I'm asking for."

Edith huffed, and then did a double take when she finally registered Violet's presence.

But instead of looking embarrassed that Violet had witnessed the spat, Edith lifted an accusatory finger and pointed at Cain. "Tell him," she ordered Violet. "Tell him he can't go."

"I'll do no such thing," Violet said quietly.

Edith started to nod in agreement, then her lips parted in shock when she registered Violet's words. It was a toss-up who was more surprised: Edith or Cain.

"The interviews are next week," Edith said, her voice more pleading than angry now. "We haven't even begun to prepare. I've managed to sweet-talk some of the board members' assistants into giving me the questions he'll be asked, but—"

"So give me the questions," Cain said. "I can read them on the plane."

"That's not the same as practicing or having someone to explain each person's idiosyncrasies."

"Well, it'll have to be good enough, Edith," Cain said gently, his tone surprisingly patient. "Because I didn't come here to ask your permission, just the courtesy of letting you know in person that I'll be gone until Wednesday."

Edith made a low sound of irritation, and Violet couldn't help but smile, because it wasn't a noise she'd heard Edith make before, but it was still familiar. She wondered if Cain realized how much he resembled his grandmother in this moment.

Edith's gaze snapped to Violet, and she quickly wiped the smile off her face, but not before Edith's expression turned speculative. She looked back at her grandson.

"Take Violet with you," Edith commanded.

"*What?*" Violet and Cain said at the same time.

Edith was already nodding, as though the decision was final. "Violet knows all the board members. With her insights, you'll have them eating out of your hand."

"I don't want them eating out of my hand. And it's Mardi Gras, Edith. Even if I *wanted* to spend it doing mock interviews, and I don't, there's no chance of finding a hotel room within fifty miles this late in the game."

"So, she can stay at your place."

"Hell no," Cain snapped.

Violet looked away quickly so he wouldn't see how much the swiftness of his rejection hurt.

He saw it anyway, and swore under his breath.

"My place is small, Duchess," he said gruffly. "I'd sleep on the couch, but we'd still be sleeping in the same room. You'd have no privacy."

I wouldn't mind.

"Don't be an uptight prude, Cain," Edith said.

Violet let out a startled laugh, and Cain gave both women a dark look.

"I'm not a prude," he said, running a hand through his hair in aggravation. "I'm just saying I'll be working most of the time. What would you even do?"

"She's a big girl, she can entertain herself," Edith persisted.

"She can also speak for herself," Violet cut in.

Edith opened her mouth, irritated at the interruption, then nodded. "Of course. Tell Cain you want to go to New Orleans."

Violet shook her head in amusement at the older woman's high-handedness. Then she looked at Cain. "I want to go to New Orleans."

"See," Cain said, throwing up his arms in triumph as he turned to Edith. "She—"

Then he turned back to Violet, stunned. "*What?*"

She shrugged as though she hadn't just dropped a bombshell, shocking everyone in the room, including herself. Especially herself. But the more she sat with the decision, the better it felt. "I've never been. I'd like to see it."

He looked skeptical. "It's dirty, and wild, and loud. Especially at Mardi Gras."

Violet laughed. "Wow, way to sell it. I thought you loved your city."

"It's the best place on earth," he said without hesitation. "Also the best *jazz* on earth."

"Hey." She lifted a finger in mock warning. "Easy. New York holds that title."

"You can't say that if you've never even been to New Orleans."

Violet raised her eyebrows in victory; he'd just walked right into the wrong side of his argument.

"She has you there," Edith told Cain gleefully.

He slowly turned and gave his grandmother a pointed look, though there was a playful note to his glare that was almost touching.

Edith cleared her throat. "I think I'll go have Alvin make me a cocktail."

She set her hand fondly on Cain's forearm as she passed, patting it once, and Violet's heart squeezed when he placed his own upon it for a moment.

With Edith out of the room, Cain turned back to Violet. "You seriously want to do this?"

"Let's just say I'm overdue for a vacation. And I'm *really* overdue for a little spontaneous living. But"—she nodded in the direction Edith had gone—"you do realize she's playing us, right?"

Cain stepped toward her, sliding an arm around her waist and pressing his palm against her lower back to tug her forward. "Nobody makes me do anything I don't want to do, Duchess."

His head dipped down to hers, close enough so she could feel his breath on her lips, close enough to make her ache.

Then he released her and stepped back. "Go home and pack. Flight's tomorrow morning at nine."

Twenty

Violet sat in her first-class seat and tried desperately not to fidget. Or cry.

She pressed her palms together in her lap and stared hard at them as she ran the pad of her right thumb over her left nail. Then the pad of her left over her right nail.

And repeat. Repeat. Repeat. Repeat.

The plane hit a patch of turbulence, and her fingers moved faster, pressing harder and harder, palms sweaty, heart racing.

"Duchess. What the hell are you doing?"

Her head snapped up, dismayed to see that Cain had quit whatever he was reading and was watching her.

"Sorry. I always think one of these days I'll get better—"

The plane gave a sudden jolt to the left before righting

again, but not before she panicked and reached out to grab the closest thing for stability: Cain's forearm.

His expression softened in understanding. "Nervous flyer?"

She managed a jerky nod, not quite ready to remove her hand from his arm. And even though she was fairly certain her nails were gouging into his skin through the fabric of his thin sweater, he didn't shake her off.

Cain reached up and hit the button to summon the flight attendant, who appeared seconds later with a smile. "You need something?"

"We changed our minds about those drinks," Cain told the woman with a quick smile. "Two glasses of wine. One red, one white."

"Of course."

"It's not even noon," Violet said, squeezing her eyes shut and trying to get it together.

"I know what time it is." He set his hand over hers, gently pressing down until her hand was flattened against him, her palm settling against the soft fabric of the blue sweater. She relaxed slightly at the calming pressure. Enough to open her eyes.

The flight attendant appeared with two glasses of wine, setting them both on Cain's tray table.

He handed Violet the white. She took a small sip, then stared absently at the pale yellow liquid.

"I hate flying," she said needlessly.

He said nothing, merely sipped his own wine and watched her.

She set her wine on his table, her hand going to her pearls. "Flying always takes me back to my parents' death. It was a helicopter, not a plane, but when I'm a million feet in the air, it doesn't seem to make a difference."

"Tell me about them."

Violet sipped the wine, feeling a bit steadier, happy for the distraction. "They were *fun*. Not lax—they expected me to mind my manners, do my homework, get good grades, and all that. But my house was always the one my friends wanted to go to after school. I took it for granted at the time, but looking back, I remember a lot of laughter. My parents seemed to genuinely love being married." She stared out the window. "Sometimes I wonder if they loved being married more than they loved being parents."

"You've mentioned they traveled a lot?"

Violet nodded. "They lived for it. They didn't always leave me behind, but . . ." She shrugged. "I spent a lot of time at my grandmother's even before they died."

Her hand lifted to her necklace.

His gaze dropped to her hand as it fiddled with the necklace. "The pearls. They were your mother's?"

Violet nodded. "They were the most conservative thing about her. She wore them almost every day. Except when they went on one of their 'adventures.' That's what they always called them. Not trips, not vacations. Adventures. She left her pearls with me. Told me to watch over them until she got back." Her hand dropped. "And then one day she didn't come back."

The plane gave another sharp bump that had her instinctively reaching a hand toward Cain again.

"Easy," he murmured, catching her hand with his and giving it a quick squeeze. "You're all right, Duchess."

"I know." *Sort of.* She shut her eyes.

He squeezed her hand once more, then released it, setting his wine on the small surface between their seats.

He went to unbuckle his seat belt, but she grabbed his wrist in panic. "The fasten seat belt sign is still on!"

"I'll be quick," he said with a wink.

He was. He stood and opened the overhead compartment to quickly retrieve his small duffel bag before sitting again and refastening his seat belt, all without the flight attendant noticing.

Violet took another sip of wine as he pulled out an iPad and earbuds. He set the iPad on its stand on his tray table and, unwinding the headphones, stuck one in her left ear before she could register what was happening.

She pulled it out. "What are you doing?"

"Better question is what are *we* doing?" he said, turning on the iPad and putting the other earbud in his right year.

"Fine. What are we doing?"

"Watching a movie. To get your mind off the whole up-in-the-air thing."

"Oh, I don't think—" She broke off as she noticed the movie he'd picked. "*The Princess and the Frog*?"

"A classic."

"I've never seen it."

"It's good," he said in a matter-of-fact tone. "And set in Louisiana, so it's required watching for you before we land."

She stared at him, waiting for more explanation. "Okay, you know you have to explain, right? You're literally the last person I'd expect to be familiar with Disney movies."

He shrugged. "My best friend has a seven-year-old girl. I babysat before they moved to Germany."

"Best friend? Germany?"

"Yes, I have one, Duchess. Clay's in the army. Stationed in Frankfurt."

The plane hit another bout of turbulence, and Cain wordlessly extended his hand, palm up. Slowly, Violet rested her hand on his, as the trademark Disney castle appeared on-screen.

Halfway through the movie, the pilot finally found some smoother air, and the turbulence stopped.

Cain did not release her hand.

"I've never seen anything quite like it," Violet said in awe.

She stood on the tiny Juliet balcony of Cain's apartment and took in the surrounding French Quarter.

Everything felt so *alive*. New York was alive too, but in a bustling, busy sort of way. New Orleans was somehow both lush and vibrant, yet unhurried. As though the city itself had a pulse.

"The architecture is so uniquely beautiful. Everything looks a bit like a fairy tale," she said, looking over her shoulder at Cain.

Cain was leaning against the open French doors, watching her. "You may want to wait until Tuesday before making that assessment."

"What's Mardi Gras like?"

"Insane. Fantastic."

"I can't wait," she said, inhaling the faint smell of what must be a nearby bakery. "I love this place already."

"Sorry we didn't have any luck finding a hotel room."

"You warned me it would be impossible," she said. "And it's me who should be apologizing. I'm crashing your space."

"And there's not a lot of it."

There wasn't. Cain's apartment, as he'd prepared her for, was small. There was no door separating the bedroom from the main living space. The kitchen was more of a wall than a room, with a basic two-burner stove and a tired-looking fridge. The counter had enough room for a coffeepot, and that was about it.

The living room was a couch, a chair, and a chest he used as a coffee table. There was a small, scuffed wooden dining table tucked into the corner and two chairs, both looking like they wobbled.

And then there was the bed. Not a huge, enormous king bed, but one that tucked into the slightly slanted ceiling, an unfussy gray quilt. The bed where she'd be sleeping.

With him just a few feet away.

He caught her eyes, and she wondered if he was thinking the same thing.

Then he disappeared, and when he came back, he was holding two standard drinking glasses, both filled with sparkling liquid.

"Champagne."

"Sure, we can call it that," he said, handing it to her. "Just as long as you adjust your taste buds to prepare for something I believe an ex-girlfriend picked up for nine bucks."

"Ex-girlfriend?" she asked. "What was her name?"

"Jolie."

"Of course it was. How long did you date?"

"Not long. Few weeks. Burned bright and then she moved to Birmingham to take care of her grandma. I wished her well. End of story."

"Well, *that's* not very juicy."

"Not much of my romantic history is."

"Probably more so than mine," she muttered.

He looked up quickly, then back at the bottle. "What happened with you and the duke?"

"We broke up."

Cain handed her a glass. "Yeah, I got that part. Why?"

She sniffed her drink as she considered her answer. It

smelled vaguely of banana, which was probably not a good sign.

"I guess I realized he wasn't what I wanted anymore," Violet said softly.

Cain nodded without saying anything, and Violet didn't know if she was relieved or disappointed that he hadn't ask what she *did* want.

"Are you nervous?" she asked him.

"About what?"

"The vote."

Cain took his time answering, joining her on the balcony, and resting his forearms on the railing.

Then his head dropped forward as he exhaled, and he turned his head slightly to look at her. "I want it, Duchess."

"Well, sure," she said softly. "Why else would you have put yourself through all this?"

"No, I mean . . ." He looked away again. "I really want it."

"You sound surprised."

"I am," he admitted. "When it all started, I wanted it for the obvious reasons. The money. The prestige. Probably a little bit of ego. And honestly, I'm not entirely sure I didn't want to try and fail, just to stick it to Edith."

"Plus," he added, looking over at her, "there was no way I was going to let the snotty princess with her pearls and dismissive gaze be the one to run me off."

"I deserve that," Violet said. "I was horrible to you that day in Edith's parlor."

"I didn't exactly play the part of white knight myself."

She laughed. "Have you ever?"

He looked away quickly, but not before she saw the flash of hurt that made her chest ache with regret.

"Hey." She touched his arm. "I didn't mean that."

He gently slid his arm from beneath her hand. "Sure you did. It's fine."

"Cain—"

"So, yes," he said, a little too loud. "I want the job."

Reluctantly, Violet let him shift the conversation.

"Why?" she asked, to urge him on. She sensed he needed to talk it out, even if he wasn't entirely comfortable doing so.

He took a distracted sip of the drink. "The damn place got under my skin more than I expected. I thought it would be just pushing papers around a huge desk and signing contracts nobody needed me to read, but there's a hell of a lot more to it."

"And you enjoy it."

He looked like he wanted to protest, then nodded. "Shit. Yeah. I think I do, it's just . . ."

"What?"

He tugged at his ear, looking impatient. "It doesn't feel right."

"What? The role? You can grow into it, and—"

"That's just it. Shouldn't I have to grow into it before it's offered to me? Shouldn't I have to earn it?"

He sounded so impassioned that Violet didn't know what to say in response.

"And let's face it, I'm never going to be the guy you're trying to make me. The one who actually chooses to wear a suit when he doesn't have to. Who gets his hair cut every three weeks at a place that serves cappuccinos. I hate museums, I think caviar tastes like shit, and I can't for the life of me figure out what the hell people do on yachts."

She smiled. "They eat caviar and talk about museums."

He laughed. "Fuck. See?"

"So maybe you'll be your own kind of CEO," she said. "Break the mold. Create your own."

"That's not what Edith wants," he said, tilting his glass up. "That's not what . . ." He took a drink.

"That's not what?" Violet urged.

"That's not what people want from the job. It's not what they're signing up for."

Violet frowned, feeling like she was missing something, that there was something he wasn't explaining.

"How do you think the vote on Friday will go?" she asked.

"No clue."

"What's your gut say?"

Cain stared down at the busy streets for a long minute, thinking.

"Long shot," he answered finally. "I haven't been playing kiss ass trying to convince them I should get it, and your boy

Keith's basically had his lips glued to the board's butt trying to convince them that I shouldn't."

He lifted his glass again, then scowled down at it without taking a sip. "This is piss."

"It's gross," she agreed. "I thought I saw some beer in the fridge."

Cain smiled. "Beer, Duchess?"

"I liked it well enough the other night. When you kissed me," she said boldly.

Cain's smile slipped, and he straightened. She held her breath, hoping he'd take the hint, and when his eyes lingered on her mouth, she thought he had.

But then he eased away from her and headed back into the apartment. "Beer it is. We can drink them while we rehearse for those damn interviews."

Twenty-One

"Why does everything in this city taste so *good*?" Violet asked, looking down at the food on the table, trying to decide if she could possibly fit in another bite, and if so, what it would be.

"Even the fried oysters?" Cain gave her a half smile over his cocktail—a Sazerac, which was apparently a New Orleans classic, but not one to Violet's liking. She'd tried a sip, but stuck to her usual white wine. "I thought you said they were an *abomination*."

"That was before I had them," she admitted. "You win. They're delicious that way."

She'd happily let Cain lead her way out of her comfort zone over the course of the meal. There wasn't a vegetable or salad in sight, at least half of what they'd consumed had been deliciously fried, and she'd even tried *alligator*.

Each bite was more enjoyable than the last.

"You might want to save room," Cain said. "We haven't had dessert."

"No way." She shook her head decisively, a hand on her stomach. "I can't."

"You can, and you will." He gave her a crooked smile. "Not here. But I know a place."

She looked at her watch. "That's still open?"

"New York's not the only city that never sleeps."

"It's strange, isn't it?" she mused. "That the two cities can have so many similarities and yet be so different."

"A bit like people."

She gave him a surprised glance. "That's a whimsical thought."

He grimaced and lowered his voice to cowboy grunts. "Football. Beer. Steak."

Violet laughed. "I get it. Very masculine. But you've been right about your city. There's something magical about New Orleans, isn't there?"

"Yes." He didn't hesitate.

Violet watched him. "You love it here."

"Sure. It's my home."

The statement was delivered off-the-cuff, an instinctive response on his part, but it made the food in Violet's stomach churn unpleasantly. "And New York is not."

He took his time answering. "No."

She studied him. "If you get the job at Rhodes, you'd

have to be in New York. You'd give up your home? Walk away from New Orleans?"

Cain looked frustrated. "Sure. Yeah. Life's full of sacrifices."

"What if you don't get the job?" she pressed. "Will you still return to New Orleans?"

He met her gaze steadily. "Yeah, Duchess. I will."

She forced a smile, understanding what he was trying to tell her, albeit more kindly than she'd have expected of the man she met a month ago: *Without the job, there's nothing to keep me in NYC.*

"All right," she said a bit too brightly. "Let's see if this dessert place is as good as you say."

Violet reached over to her purse and pulled out her wallet, but Cain snatched it out of her fingers and tucked it back into her bag. "Nope."

"Let's at least split it."

"My turf, my rules, sweetheart."

Sweetheart.

Violet liked the way it rolled off his tongue, even as she was aware he'd probably said it to plenty of women, perhaps in this very restaurant.

Not liking the thought, she distracted herself by looking around the restaurant, which was a pleasant blend of modern and timeless. "I like this place."

"But?" he asked expectantly.

"No *but.*"

Cain looked skeptical. "Really? You're not going to point out that the lopsided table, the lack of a tablecloth, the paper napkins?"

"No! I wasn't going to say any of that," she said, feeling a little stung.

"My mistake," he said, idly swirling his drink. "You're more accepting of my town than I was of yours."

"Yes," she agreed. "I am. Though I'd like to note, New York does have Central Park. Hard to beat that."

"New Orleans has cemeteries."

She blinked. "*That's* the selling point you want to go with? Burial grounds?"

"Trust me. They're worth seeing. I think there are tours; something for you to do while I'm at work tomorrow?"

Violet actually had every intention of going to work with him tomorrow, but she knew he'd put up an immediate protest, and didn't want to ruin their evening with an argument, so she merely gave a noncommittal smile.

He finished his drink and took out his wallet, pulling out plenty of bills and tucking them under his plate. He came around to her chair, tugged it backward. "C'mon. I'm about to blow your mind."

Violet laughed. "All right. But I'm skeptical that anything will beat those corn muffin things dipped in the saucy stuff we just had."

Cain shook his head and took her hand in his to haul her

to her feet before releasing her, a bit too soon for her liking. "Oh, Duchess. Prepare to eat your words."

"Well?" Cain asked, leaning back against the rickety chair and shooting her a cocky grin.

"I *would* eat my words," Violet said, closing her eyes as she chewed. "But I'm too busy eating these. They have to be made in heaven."

"Quite possibly. N'awlins lesson number one, never underestimate the mighty beignet."

Violet opened her eyes to see him reach for another, eating his in two large bites.

"I can't believe how crowded this place is at this time of night," Violet said, taking a sip of her café au lait and looking around.

"You should see it in the morning," Cain said. "Plenty of people, tourists especially, treat it like their morning coffee and doughnut run. We locals know late night is where it's at." He winked.

"Unusual that a place would have a tourist *and* a local crowd. In Manhattan, it's usually one or the other. Times Square with its glut of out-of-towners, or the hole-in-the-wall with six tables, tucked into the West Village, where the bartender knows everyone's name."

"Well, let's not forget I'm *with* a tourist," Cain said,

smiling. "But there was no way I could let you come to New Orleans for the first time and not experience Café du Monde."

"I think I'd come here even if I lived here," Violet said firmly. Then she narrowed her eyes at his expression. "What. What was that look?"

He smiled slightly. "Nothing. I just believe you *would* come here."

"Why do you sound so surprised? These beignets are the best thing I've ever tasted."

"Not surprised that you love beignets. Surprised that you're so decisive." He hesitated slightly, then looked up again. "You've changed, Duchess."

"Have I?" she asked lightly. "How?"

He leaned forward, capturing her eyes with his. "The woman I first met was a blank slate that anyone could write on to suit their own agenda. The woman sitting across from me now . . . she knows what she wants."

"I do know what I want." She licked powdered sugar off her thumb and held his gaze boldly. "I'm even prepared to go for it."

His gaze tracked the motion of her thumb. Lingered on her mouth. "Knowing what you want for breakfast—or dessert—that's the easy part. I'm talking life stuff, Duchess. Big stuff."

"I know what you're talking about, Cain. And like I said. I know what I want."

He sat back, his expression more careful now. "And what is that?"

Violet took her time responding, glancing around at the couples feeding each other bits of beignet. The fussy kids up way past their bedtime. The middle-aged woman sitting alone and looking perfectly content to be so. The old men sipping coffee and laughing at what she liked to think was a bawdy joke.

"I was never one of those kids who boldly proclaimed they wanted to be a doctor or lawyer or the president," she said, because it felt like a logical place to start explaining.

"Christ," Cain said with a startled laugh. "What the hell sort of kids did you hang out with? My dreams started and ended with working at IHOP so I could have pancakes whenever I wanted."

"At least that's *something*. I mean, at least you knew you liked pancakes. I didn't even have that! I always just sort of thought I'd figure out who I was, but I never really did."

"Not even in college? Isn't that when you rich kids are supposed to figure that shit out?"

"I majored in sociology."

He shook his head, indicating the word meant nothing to him, and she explained. "The study of human behavior, society, culture. I loved it, I still find it fascinating, but in terms of turning into a passion, a vocation, a career . . ."

She lifted her shoulders and let them drop.

"So, how'd you go from that to working for Edith?"

"Because she needed me," Violet said automatically, then just as quickly, corrected herself. "No, that's not quite right. I tell myself that, but I think I needed her more than she needed me. She knew that. Gave me a purpose."

"She's needed you," Cain said. "Maybe not as her assistant or whatever the hell you've been doing for her. But she needs you like you need her."

"Because neither of us have family."

"Because you *are* family," he said firmly.

Violet felt her eyes water a little, not realizing how much she'd needed someone to tell her that.

"Plus," Violet said lightly, looking up once she'd gotten her emotions under control, "who knows if she has some *other* secret, surly grandsons to be whipped into shape?"

"Impossible," Cain said confidently. "I'm one of a kind." He picked up another beignet, studying it with a slight frown before taking a bite. "So you'd do it over again?"

"Do what?"

"Go along with Edith's request to, how did you phrase it? Whip me into shape?"

Violet didn't hesitate. "No. I wouldn't."

He looked up. "Been that bad, has it?"

"No." Violet's voice was soft. "And even hypothetically, I hate the thought of saying no to Edith when she needs something from me. She's wanted so badly for the company to stay in the family, and I want that for her, because I love her. But she shouldn't have asked you to change. And I shouldn't have agreed to help."

His gaze dropped again, though he didn't acknowledge her statement as he took a bite of the beignet and chewed thoughtfully.

"Okay, so you don't want to be a lawyer or the president, and don't have any use for your college degree. You've got another vision for your life?"

"I want a family," Violet said with so much confidence in her tone that he paused chewing for a second. "I want a husband who adores me. I want kids. Three, maybe more. I want to take them to Central Park, push strollers while walking a big golden retriever that worships a very skeptical Coco. When the kids are older, I want to go on picnics where everyone fights over the last chocolate chip cookie, so we split it. I want my daughter to pester Edith about tips on taking over the business, I want my son to love piano . . . For that matter, *I* want to learn how to play the piano, but I'm probably too old," she said jokingly.

He shook his head. "Disagree."

"You've heard my version of 'Heart and Soul.' I don't remember you falling all over yourself at my talent," Violet teased.

"Speaking of piano," he said, reaching out and tilting the watch on her wrist toward him. "We've got to go if we want to catch the 2 a.m. set."

"Oh, right," she said with an affected bored tone. "This jazz you claim rivals New York City's scene."

"Duchess, you're not just about to discover jazz headquarters—you're about to see its birthplace."

Cain hauled her to her feet as he had at the restaurant, only this time he stayed close a moment longer, his eyes searching her face. "You deserve it."

"What, to learn piano?" she joked.

He didn't smile back. "All of it. You deserve to have everything you want, Duchess."

Twenty-Two

*After a solid thirty minutes of badgering and threatening to drop his coffeepot off the balcony if he didn't concede, Violet had eventually gotten her way and convinced Cain to let her tag along on his workday.

So far, Cain's workplace was everything he'd promised: loud, intense, and a bit overwhelming. The warehouse—actually, more like a *compound* of warehouses—was simply enormous. There were forklifts backing up in every direction, workers shouting greetings and orders at one another, and yet even to Violet's untrained eye, she could see it was organized chaos.

There were no near-collisions, supervisors wearing red vests and carrying tablets oversaw every movement, and as far as she could tell, the constant crisscross of pallets of tomatoes, iced seafood, loaves of packaged bread, and stacks of linens all made it onto the right trucks.

The strict organization, the lack of mistakes, the general worker satisfaction and good moods had a source too: *Cain.*

She'd known he was the co-owner, but she hadn't known what that meant. Hadn't realized, until a chatty group of workers on their break had brought her up to speed that one of the owners was the figurehead, the man whose name was on the Parker Distribution sign out front. Cain, though, ran the show. She'd learned that apart from the last month when he'd taken "personal leave," he was the sort of boss who put in longer hours than his employees. He was the guy who was always around, ready to lend a hand loading trucks when they were short a man, and the boss who was there to listen to an employee having an off day because he'd had to put his dog to sleep. He ironed out arguments, took out the trash, and made the tough call when a food delivery came in short and they had to decide between delivering the limited inventory to a longtime small customer or their brand-new big customer.

Violet hadn't doubted for a second that Cain was competent. She'd known within a day of meeting him that he was more observant and quick thinking than he wanted people to know.

But she hadn't expected him to be so *revered.*

Most disturbingly of all, she'd never paused to think that maybe he missed it or that he loved his work.

And it was increasingly obvious that he *did* love it.

She'd felt his excitement during the car ride when he'd hummed along with the music and in his buzzing energy as they'd pulled through the gated security fence.

And it wasn't just the work. It was in the way he'd instantly relaxed when he'd stepped back into his apartment. The passion in his voice when he pointed out lingering signs of the Hurricane Katrina tragedy, and the almost boyish energy when he tried to sell her on the fried oysters and the city's jazz.

Which, to his credit, had been every bit as good as promised, even if she was paying the price this morning with only a couple of hours of sleep.

Violet started to make her way back to the main office space, and several wrong turns and requests for directions later, she let herself into the reception area, where the receptionist was typing and talking on the phone at the same time. She gave Violet a distracted smile, then returned to explaining the impracticalities of a Sunday evening crawfish delivery.

Violet intended to settle in the waiting area with the book Cain suggested she bring, but she slowed when she heard Cain's laugh and noticed one of the doors was open. She didn't mean to snoop; she was just curious. The room had a small window, the miniblinds open just enough to make out Cain leaning back in a chair, booted feet up on a desk and laughing with a short, stocky woman standing in front of a white board.

Neither of them noticed her lurking.

"I'm seriously so sorry—"

"I swear to God, Megs, if you apologize one more time, you're fired," Cain said with a grin.

"I'm—" The woman huffed. "Fine. I'm just pissed with myself. You trusted me with everything. It was going so well, it's just . . . *fuck* Mardi Gras. It's like the hotels and restaurants don't know it comes every year."

Cain laughed. "Told you. But don't beat yourself up. Your first one was always going to suck, and I screwed you over extra hard by ditching town in a year when it fell so early."

"You're allowed to have a life, boss."

Cain had been tossing a mini basketball from hand to hand, but for a moment, he held it in his right hand and just stared at it with a frown. "I'm allowed to have a life, yes. I'm just afraid I walked away from it."

"I disagree," Megs said, sitting down across from him. "You're just discovering a new part of it. A family member you didn't know existed showed up, and you've got to explore that."

He resumed tossing the ball, adding a little more snap to the motion than before. "What if *this* is my family? I've got a thousand people on my payroll, and that's not counting the wives and husbands. You, Amy, the twins."

"Amy and the boys *do* miss you," she admitted. "Jamie, in particular, has been a nightmare because his new piano teacher is trying to force him to learn Beethoven, who you told him is boring."

"Whoops." Cain grinned, unrepentant.

"But we'll be here. And if you decide to move to New York for good, we'll visit. I mean, the Lego store alone." She studied him. "Are you moving? For good?"

"Not up to me. I don't even know if I'll get the job."

"They'd be idiots not to know that if you can come in here and untangle the Mardi Gras mess I made in a couple hours, you can run anything. But in case they are a bunch of fools and you don't get it . . . you'll be back?"

Violet held her breath.

The ball tossing slowed. "I dunno. Maybe. Probably."

Violet's heart sank just a little, even though she wasn't surprised.

"Nothing to keep me there if I don't get the job," Cain continued.

Her heart sank a little further.

"What about your grandmother?"

Cain grunted.

"And maybe . . . the girl?" Megs said in a taunting tone. "Violet's sweet. And gorgeous."

"Megs. Shut up."

"What's that I'm hearing?" She lifted a hand to her ear. "Definitely not a denial, that's for sure."

The ball stopped again, this time because Cain tossed it at his manager, who batted it away with a laugh.

Biting her lip, Violet quietly crept away, a jumble of confused emotions.

Twenty-Three

"Come on," Violet said, reaching toward Cain's neck for the beads, then laughing when he grabbed her wrist. "You're not going to give me a single strand? You're wearing, like, fifty."

"You know how this works, Duchess." He pointed to a group of giggling women who lifted their shirts and were rewarded with a dozen strands tossed at their feet from one of the balconies above.

"And I told *you*, it's watered-down prostitution to show your boobs in exchange for jewelry."

"Huh, I'm sorry you feel that way," he said with sham regret as he twirled the beads on his finger.

"How'd *you* get so many?" she accused.

"Earned 'em."

Proving his point, Cain turned to one of the balconies,

which was crowded with middle-aged women, and yanked up his shirt. The women whooped and ogled.

Violet didn't whoop. She did ogle.

Beads rained down at Cain's feet as he laughed and pulled his shirt down. "See what happens when you put out?"

"Pathetic."

"Come on. You only live once, Duchess. What if this is your only Mardi Gras? It's a Bourbon Street tradition."

Violet chewed her lip. "I'm not wearing a cute bra."

"I've seen worse."

"Gosh, thanks. Wait, how have you seen *this* one?"

"We're sharing a room," he pointed out.

"Yes, but I purposefully waited until you went into the bathroom to shower before changing." She crossed her arms and gave him a playful glare.

"Huh. The door must have cracked open." He didn't look the least bit apologetic.

Old Violet might have gotten her feathers ruffled, or at least been embarrassed. New Violet was a little disappointed all he did was peek.

"So, what's it gonna be?" He nudged her, pointing up at the balcony. "You gonna earn your beads, or no?"

She bit her lip. "You can't tell Edith."

"Yes, because that was my first order of business. To tell my grandma about all the breasts I've seen."

"You called her *grandma*!" Violet said, in delight. "Usually it's *Edith* or a clipped *grandmother*."

"Fine. Whatever. Can we please not talk about her at the same time I'm trying to get a glimpse under your shirt?"

Violet looked around at the happy, slightly drunken revelry of Bourbon Street. Yesterday, Cain had told her to imagine the messiest, happiest, sloppiest party in the world, and so far the reality was surpassing every expectation. Restaurant and bar owners were handing out gold, purple, and green beads by the handfuls. The street was practically coated in them. All she had to do was pick up a couple of strands.

"If I do this, you have to promise not to peek," she said, turning back to Cain.

"Promise?" she asked when he said nothing.

"Hell no." His smile was boyish, but the heat in his eyes was masculine, and intoxicating.

Violet reveled in all the intense emotions consuming her. She felt bold. Brave. Even a little bit sexy. And while the feelings were unfamiliar, they also felt perfect, as though she'd finally uncovered her own essence.

She laughed in delight at the woman she'd uncovered in herself. The woman who had stared back at her this morning hadn't been concerned about the fact that Cain's itty-bitty bathroom made it impossible for her to do her usual hair and makeup routine. She hadn't been concerned with the way the swampy humidity made her hair frizz and makeup melt right off, or that she had bags under eyes from another late night at the jazz clubs with Cain.

She felt deliciously alive, almost giddy with excitement

to see what the next moment would bring, and she knew exactly who had brought about that change. Violet may have set out to transform Cain, but it was becoming increasingly clear that it was she who had changed.

"Okay," she said, tapping Cain's arm excitedly. "Okay, I'm going to do it."

Before Violet could second-guess herself and chicken out, she turned toward a row of balconies, and grabbing the hem of her silk T-shirt, pulled it upward, revealing her basic white bra. Then, as fast as humanly possible, she tugged it back down again, but not before she got a couple of approving whoops. She closed her eyes and laughed as a dozen strands of cheap beads landed at her feet. One even whipped her cheek, but she didn't care.

She'd never felt this giddy. This *free*. For the first time in her life, she was simply living, with zero concern as to what anyone around her thought.

"I did it," she announced gleefully, gathering up some of the beads off the ground, barely noticing they were sticky with beer and who knows what else, and placing them proudly around her neck.

At Cain's suggestion, she'd left her usual pearls carefully packed away in her suitcase for the day. She'd felt a bit lost without them at first, but as she touched the sticky, cheap plastic yellow, purple, and green strands, she smiled. It was a little nice to be a different sort of Violet, one who could simply be an adult woman who did what she wanted in the moment rather than carefully crafting every behavior to blend into the background, to ensure she never upset anyone.

Cain's knuckle gently hooked beneath her chin, tilting her face up to his. He didn't smile, but his eyes were warm. "You said your parents liked adventure."

She nodded.

"You did them proud today."

Violet laughed. "Because I flashed strangers? I don't think that's what they had in mind for me."

"I didn't say they'd want to bear witness to the actual event." Cain's smile was gentle. "Just that they'd like knowing this side of you exists. In fact, I think they do know." He pointed up.

Crap, Violet thought, her eyes welling just a little bit with tears as the realization hit her hard: she loved him.

Violet loved this stubborn, complicated, impossible-to-read, impossible-to-have man in front of her.

He was rough, and gruff, and it made the slivers of sweetness all the more meaningful.

"Hey." His finger touched a tear on her cheek. "Shit. I said something wrong."

"No. No, you said everything right," Violet said, tunneling her fingers into his hair. Then she pulled his mouth down to hers and kissed him in the middle of Bourbon Street.

Cain's arms were around her immediately, one angling

low over her hips, the other wrapping around her shoulders, pulling her roughly against his maleness.

His lips moved gently over hers, and Violet felt the chaotic scene around them fade away until she was lost in Cain's clean, soapy smell, the feel of his tongue exploring the corners of her mouth, the involuntary sound in the back of his throat when her nails scraped lightly against his neck in need.

Someone bumped into them, jarring their mouths apart with a gasp.

"Sorry!" one of the trio of giggling, tipsy girls called as they stumbled away on platform heels.

Violet was sorry too. Not that the kiss had ended, but that they weren't alone, that he wasn't kissing her everywhere.

"Don't, Duchess," Cain said with a rough laugh, his thumb pulling at the bottom of her lip, as he watched her mouth.

"Don't what?"

"Look at me like that," he said, his thumb brushing over her lip as he scowled.

Her tongue boldly touched the pad of his finger. "Why not?"

He let out a low groan. "Because my place is right around the corner. And if we go back right now, I'm going to have a hell of a time making myself sleep on the couch tonight."

"And if I didn't want you to?"

Cain's expression darkened slightly, and he moved closer,

cupping her face. "Duchess, listen to me. All those things you want. The kids, the husband, the dog. That's not my scene. You understand?"

Violet swallowed, tucking away the pain at that proclamation to be dealt with another day. If tonight was all he was offering, she'd take it.

"I understand," she said, stepping closer to him, setting a hand to his chest. "But I want other things too."

Twenty-Four

They hadn't even shut the door to Cain's apartment before he was reaching for her. His hands gripped low on her hips, tugging her middle against his as his boot kicked the door closed.

His lips trailed along her jaw, his mouth pressing hotly just below her ear, and Violet's head fell back with a moan as he trailed wet kisses over her throat. He knew just when to nip with his teeth, when to soothe with his tongue . . .

Breathless, Violet's hands roamed over his shoulders, his chest, his back, greedily exploring. If she only got the one night, she wanted all of it.

She wanted *him*.

When feeling him over his T-shirt was no longer enough, her fingers slipped beneath the hem at his waist. He grabbed her wrist. Violet gasped as she found herself pressed against the door, hands pinned on either side of her head as his mouth slammed down over hers in the kind of hard, possessive kiss she'd been waiting her entire life to experience.

Without releasing her mouth, he shifted her hands higher above her head, holding both wrists in one hand as his other slid back down her body, skimming over her side, her hip, then back up.

His hand on her breast was just the right combination of gentle and rough as he explored her shape, his thumb expertly teasing her nipple to attention through her shirt and bra until she ached with the need for more.

"Cain," she whispered against his mouth. "Please."

"Again." His breath was hot and hard against her lips.

"Please," she repeated.

He shook his head, gripping her hair. "No. My name. Say it."

"Cain," she said huskily, tilting her hips against his as she said it.

"Christ. Christ," Cain muttered as he lost control.

There was a tear of fabric as he tugged off her shirt, and she heard her bra hit the ground, his hands and mouth covering every inch of skin he exposed.

When he released her to tug off his boots, she reached for the beads around her neck, but he shook his head. "Leave them," he ordered.

Cain reached behind his head, grabbed a fistful of his

shirt, and yanked it over his head, seconds before hauling her to him.

He lifted her off the ground, her legs around his waist, his hands on her ass, mouths fused as he carried them both to the bed, then tumbled onto it.

With deft fingers, he unbuttoned her jeans, slid his hand into them. Violet cried out as he touched her, and his face buried in her neck. "God, I want you."

After a moment, he pulled her jeans down her legs, then sat back for a moment, breathing hard as his gaze skimmed her body. Violet vaguely had the thought that she should feel shy, embarrassed, but she only felt *want*. Her legs parted slightly in invitation, which Cain gladly accepted, bending his head to her breasts as his hands slid the panties over her hips and to the floor.

Her fingers tangled in his hair, holding him to her. "I'm glad you didn't cut it," she whispered. "I've dreamed of doing this."

He stilled for a moment "Have you?"

She nodded, and Cain rubbed his bearded cheek over her nipple, his hand dropping between her legs. "And this?"

She gasped. "And that. All of it. I want all of it."

His mouth lifted to hers, never breaking the kiss as he opened the nightstand drawer and pulled out a condom.

Violet helped him shove his jeans and briefs over his hips and shifted to accommodate him as he settled above her. She closed her eyes as he nudged her opening, but Cain waited, and only when she opened her eyes to meet his did he plunge inside her.

"Fuck," he said, gasping for breath as his head dipped slightly. "You are so perfect. You are so small . . ."

"Don't be gentle," Violet said, arching as she dug her nails into his back. "Don't hold back."

He wasn't. He didn't. Once again, her hands were pinned above her head, holding her body at his mercy as he thrust inside her, his gaze not leaving hers until he carried them both to the kind of shattering orgasm that made every previous sexual encounter feel completely irrelevant.

After they'd caught their breath, gotten some water, then done it all over again, Violet lay against his chest, her fingers idly combing through his chest hair, his arm around her shoulder, his fingers detangling her hair from the beads.

After a moment, she propped her chin up on his chest and looked up at him.

"What?" he asked with a wary smile.

"I think you were right."

"Probably," he said. "But when specifically?"

"Back when we first met. You rather crudely told me I looked like a woman who hadn't been properly f—"

Cain's smile dropped, and he touched his fingers to her mouth to stop her words. "Don't. Don't, Duchess. That's not what this was."

Her breath caught. "It wasn't?"

Slowly, he shook his head.

She laid her head back down, and as she drifted off into sated sleep, she could have sworn she heard him mutter, *I only wish that's all it was.*

Violet awoke on her stomach, sticky Mardi Gras beads plastered to her chest and a warm hand stroking her bare back.

"Duchess," Cain said softly. "You've gotta get up. You've got to get going if you don't want to miss your flight."

Groggily, Violet lifted her head, blinking her way through the sleep fog, then scrambling upright when she realized:

1. She'd overslept.
2. She was naked.
3. Cain was not.
4. He'd said she was going to miss *her* flight.

She fumbled around for her shirt, and remembering that it was on the floor, settled for pulling the pillow in front of her.

"Aren't you coming? I thought we were taking the same flight."

Cain shook his head. "I need to stay here another day. Wrap up a couple things."

Violet's stomach plummeted. "Oh. I could stay with you . . ."

Cain avoided her eyes. "I'll be busy most of the time. I won't have any time to entertain you."

Entertain me?

Her hurt must have shown on her face because he tiredly rubbed at his forehead. "That's not what I meant. It's just . . . pacify Edith for me, will you? Tell her I'll be back tomorrow?"

Seriously? Edith wasn't the type to be pacified, and even if she were, Cain wasn't the type to bother with the nicety.

"I can tell when I'm being placated, Cain," Violet said softly. "You really needn't bother. You warned me last night what this was. I just didn't think you'd be the one to freak out afterward."

His jaw clenched. "I'm not freaking out. I just have some business to take care of."

She nodded and didn't push him, because if she'd learned anything from the past month with this man, it was that he needed to do things his way, on his own timeline.

"All right," she said simply, scooting toward the edge of the bed and swinging her legs to the ground. "How long will it take to get to the airport? Do I have time for a shower?"

He glanced at the clock on the nightstand. "If you make it fast."

Violet nodded, then purposely dropped the pillow and strolled naked across to the bathroom, smirking a little when she heard his stifled groan.

When she came out of the bathroom a few minutes later, hair still damp, her suitcase was open on his bed, neatly packed, and he was waiting with a cup of coffee in hand. In a to-go cup.

She laughed as she shook her head and accepted the cup. "Okay, Cain. I get it."

"You get what?"

"Your sendoff is pointed, but props for being considerate too." She lifted the coffee cup.

"Look, I thought I made it clear—"

"No, no, you did," she interrupted as she tucked her toiletry bag into her suitcase, then zipped it. "No big dog, no flowers, no happily-ever-after. I heard you, and I respect it."

"Good. So long as we're on the same page." Cain nodded as he said it, though he looked more frustrated than relieved.

"Absolutely, same page." She wheeled her suitcase to the front door. "I'll call an Uber from outside."

"Duchess—"

"You don't have to explain," she said, smiling to show him she meant it. "But if I can just say one thing?"

He hesitated, then nodded warily.

"We'll do things your way, but"—Violet went to her toes and brushed her lips lightly over his—"your way seems awfully lonely."

Then Violet grabbed her coffee, her suitcase, and left Cain Stone alone with his thoughts.

Twenty-Five

*D*amn, you are pulling out some baller moves," Ashley said approvingly over lunch. "You said that? In those exact words?"

"Yup," Violet said smugly.

"Have you heard from Cain since?"

"Nope." Violet picked up her menu. "Edith mentioned that he's back, but he hasn't texted."

"He's scared," Ashley said in a confident, matter-of-fact tone.

"Of?" Violet asked skeptically.

"Of you! You should see yourself the past couple of weeks. You're like a whole other woman. Fierce and fabulous."

"I admit, I feel fierce," Violet admitted. "But I didn't realize it was that obvious. It's not like I bought myself leather pants and black lipstick. I'm still wearing the same dresses, same pearls, same lip gloss I've been wearing since college."

"Because it's the right lip gloss, and the right wardrobe for you," Ashley said. "External makeovers can't hold a candle to internal ones, and to answer your question, yes, yours shows, and I for one am all for it."

Violet smiled. "Wish you'd shared that little insight about makeovers with me *before* I tried to change Cain into a stuffy suit. I can hardly blame him for keeping me at arm's length."

"Eh." Ashley made a disagreeing noise. "I'm not sure he wasn't due for an internal makeover of his own, and perhaps your meddling in his wardrobe was just the catalyst he needed. I mean, I'm with you—the hair and the scruff suits him. But I don't believe for one second you haven't threatened that man's bachelor way of life. *That's* what he needed changed, and that's why he's terrified."

"I dunno, Ash," Violet said, setting her menu aside after deciding on the grilled cheese with bacon. "He was pretty resolute about where we stand, before and after."

"Before and after . . . ?"

Violet tried to keep her face impassive, but Ashley wasn't her best friend for nothing. She made a squealing noise. "You boinked him! Way to bury the lead!"

Violet laugh. "I did not *boink* him. I mean, I did, but let's not call it that."

Ashley's eyes were wide and delighted. "Tell me everything. I mean *everything*. It's been way too long since I've had a good . . . boink. It *was* good, right? Please say it was good."

Violet only smiled.

"Ohhh, yeah," Ashley said, drumming her fingers on the table, then pretending to clash the cymbal. "Okay, but wait, now I'm extra annoyed at him. You guys hooked up before he kicked you out?"

"He didn't kick me out, he—" Violet chewed her cheek. "Hmm. I guess he kind of did."

"Okay, okay," Ashley said, looking around for the server. "Let's order and then we'll analyze everything. In detail."

After they'd ordered and handed their menus to the servers, Ashley crossed her arms on the table and leaned forward expectantly.

"Honestly, I don't know that there's much to analyze," Violet said slowly. "I think I need to just give him time. I've known him, what, a little over a month?"

"That was enough time for you to fall in love with him," Ashley pointed out.

Violet opened her mouth, then shut it. "You can tell?"

"Sweetie, I'm your best friend. I could tell within a week of you meeting him that he was going to steal your heart."

Violet sighed, a little happy, a little melancholy. "You could have warned me."

"No way. The discovering's half the fun." She reached across the table to squeeze Violet's hand. "I'm happy for you,

Vi. You're different than you were with Keith. Like, lit from within. Glowy."

"I *feel* glowy, but also . . ." Violet pressed her fist against her chest. "Oh, God, Ash, how do people *stand* this? This thing I'm feeling: it's as terrifying as it is exhilarating, and I can't tell what's butterflies and what's nausea. What if he doesn't *ever* want me back? What if I just wait and wait and I end up in another situation like Keith? His accessory, waiting in the wings?"

"Okay, first of all, that's not going to happen. Keith and Cain aren't even the same species. Second of all, we'll figure out a plan. Find a way to, shall we say, help Cain along."

Violet smiled. "I thought you said discovering was half the fun."

"For my best friend, yeah. But I have no such loyalty to Cain, and I'm not above nudging his reluctant ass. Men are idiots when it comes to this stuff."

"Or," Violet countered, "he just plain doesn't feel the same way back. Maybe he meant what he said and our night together was just scratching an itch, or whatever."

Ashley shook her head. "If that was the case, if he was indifferent and over it, he'd have come back with you as planned, acting like nothing happened. Instead, he went into freak-out mode."

"So what do I do? How do I unfreak him out?"

"Well." Ashley sipped her water and crunched an ice cube. "I have a thought, but you're not going to like it."

"Try me."

"See! Fierce! Okay, so," Ashley set the glass aside and crossed her arms on the table. "I know I've only met the guy once, but from everything you've told me about him, one thing has always jumped out at me: you and Cain Stone are the same."

"Eh. I think you're off base on that one," Violet said.

"You have the same issues," Ashley said, clarifying. "And I say that affectionately, because we've all got them. Except me, because I am, of course, perfect."

"Of course." Violet smiled. "Okay, so what are Cain's and my 'shared issues'?"

She added the last bit with air quotes.

Her friend's tone was gentle. "You both think you have to be something other than you are in order to be worthy of love."

Violet stared at her. "Ouch."

"I didn't say you *are* unworthy of love, just that you *think* you are."

Ashley leaned forward. "Vi, when we were kids, you were the most fearless, outspoken girl on the playground. Do you remember that? You were the one who took the slide head-first, who pushed the swing higher and higher, who called out bullies on their crap. And then your parents died, and you changed. And who could blame you? But you transformed yourself into exactly what you thought your grandmother wanted. Someone meek and perfect."

"I was afraid she wouldn't want to keep me otherwise," Violet whispered.

Ashley reached across the table and squeezed her hand. "And when your grandmother died, and Edith stepped in, you became what *she* wanted. Heck, I swear sometimes you even try to be what *I* want, even though I love all versions of you."

"You're not wrong," Violet said slowly. "But Cain's not like me. He's practically the opposite, going out of his way to be what people don't want him to be."

"Are you sure?" Ashley asked softly. "Put yourself in his shoes. One day he's just going about his life, the next his long-lost relative shows up and wants to hand him the keys to the castle. But only if he changes the way he looks, thinks, acts, dresses . . . If you were Cain, wouldn't you be wondering just a little bit which version the beautifully elegant Violet Townsend really wanted?"

Violet squeezed her eyes in regret, because her friend was right. Cain had all but called her out for as much, though he'd been more crude about it.

"Oh, God," Violet muttered. "I literally took him shopping our first day together. The things I've said to him . . . What do I do?"

"I know you're trying to give him his space, and that's generally a good plan. But in this case? Maybe you should let Cain know how you feel about him before the results of that vote. Let him know you love him. Just as he is."

Twenty-Six

*V*iolet entered the Rhodes International lobby, as she had hundreds of times in the past to see either Edith or Keith.

She tried very hard not to think about the fact that if this didn't go the way that she hoped, it could very well be the last time she would be in this building. Once Edith retired, she'd have no reason to come to this part of town to see her. And if the board voted in Cain . . .

Well, that was another worry for another day.

For now, Violet focused on the mission at hand.

Since she was on the security desk's approved list, they let her through without question, probably assuming she was expected.

Only when Violet stepped off the elevator to the executive floor did she realize she had no idea which office they'd given Cain, which meant she'd have to hunt him down. But Keith had mentioned it was a corner office, and one was Edith's, which at least narrowed her options down to three.

After waving hello to the longtime receptionist, Violet made her way around the office, greeting familiar faces by name, asking after kids and spouses. Dan Bogan was in the northeastern corner office, and Violet was on her way to check the southeastern one when she realized her mistake.

She had to walk right past another office:

Keith's.

Whose door was open. Who was staring directly at her in surprise.

"Violet?" he called through the open door, his confusion plain. "What are you doing here?"

Ugh. She hadn't seen or spoken to him since he'd groveled at Jenny and Mike's party, and she was slightly ashamed of how little she'd missed him, how seldom she even thought of him.

But since she had no way to avoid conversation without being horribly rude in front of the Rhodes employees who were pretending not to watch the interaction, Violet pasted a smile on her face and stepped inside his familiar, sterile office.

"Hi, Keith. How are you?"

"Good, good. Been busy. You're looking great. Are you here to see Edith?"

"I—" *Hmm.* As she quickly debated whether a little

white lie would be in order to save his feelings, she felt eyes on her and realized Keith wasn't alone.

"Oh, I'm so sorry," she said, turning toward the tall, dark-haired man standing off to her right. "I hadn't realized Keith was in a meeting—"

Her mouth dropped open when the man's brown eyes met hers. "Cain?"

His jaw ticked. "Duchess."

She could only stare at him. He was the same, but . . . not.

"You—your hair . . . your beard . . ."

"Thought the interviews might go better if I wasn't looking like, a . . ." He glanced at Keith. "Lumberjack, was it?"

Keith held up his hands. "Nothing personal, Cain. No hard feelings."

"Of course not," Cain said, equally affable, almost charming.

Violet frowned.

When had he learned *that* tone. It sounded nothing like the man she knew.

And then the truth hit her, uncomfortable and sharp: her. He'd learned it from her. That placid, modulated, *reveal-nothing* voice was hers.

Guilt and regret made her stomach churn. Where was the refreshing bluntness? The unabashed honesty? Had the Cain she'd fallen for disappeared along with his beard?

Unable to sort out her thoughts, she could only stare at Cain, struggling to reconcile this clean-cut man with *her* man.

"Violet," Keith said with a little laugh. "You're gawking at the man like he's an animal in the zoo."

"Isn't that what this has been all along?" Cain asked, spreading his arms wide. "Getting me ready for display, making sure I'm worth the price of admission?"

Violet felt outright nauseous now. Ashley had been horribly right. Cain *did* think his worth was dependent on him changing everything that made him *him*.

"Hey, for what it's worth, I think you look good, man," Keith told Cain with surprising friendliness, which was a warning sign in itself. "Like Clark Kent without the glasses."

Realizing her eyes were blurred with tears, Violet quickly turned and left Keith's office before the men could see her cry. Keith called her name, but she ignored him.

She kept walking until she got to her original destination, saw from the plaque on the door that the southeast corner office was indeed Cain's. Since she knew he wasn't inside, she entered, shutting the door with a little sob.

Her hopes of privacy were dashed when the door was shoved open again almost immediately by a very angry-sounding Cain. "What the hell was that about?"

For the first time in her adult life, Violet made no attempt to modulate the turbulent emotions whirling inside of her. She spun toward him, and half shouted: "I don't *want* Clark Kent without glasses." She wiped at the tears streaking her cheek, then jabbed a finger in the direction of his clean-shaven face. "I *hate* that."

"Jesus, Duchess," he muttered, rubbing his hand over his jaw. "You sure know how to gut a guy. Is it that bad?"

She choked out a laugh. "No. It's just . . . You're just . . ."

Violet held her breath, then let it out slowly. "I wish I'd told you before you changed . . . you're good enough, Cain. As you are. And that it doesn't matter to me if you get the job or not." *I'll still love you.*

Violet lost her nerve and didn't add the last part, but perhaps he heard what she didn't say aloud, because a look of fierce emotion washed over his face before he walked to her with purpose and cupped her face.

His thumbs brushed over her cheeks, wiping at the tears, then he bent his head, capturing her mouth with a searing kiss that stole her breath and her senses.

Cain's lips moved urgently over hers, both tender and desperate, and her mouth responded immediately, as though she'd spent a lifetime kissing this man.

Violet wrapped her arms around his neck, pouring everything she couldn't say into the kiss. He groaned at her response, gliding his hands down her back and pulling her closer as his mouth slid down to her neck. "Duchess," he murmured against her throat. "Duchess . . ."

Violet's fingers tangled in his hair, missing the length only for a second before deciding she liked the spiky feel against her palms just as much, found the touch of his bare cheek against her throat as erotic as the beard had been.

It was *him* she wanted. Scruffy, bald, tall, short, standing, sitting, it didn't matter, as long as it was Cain.

His hands came up to the front of her dress before he stepped back with a reluctant groan. "I have never hated the fact that this place has windows for walls as much as I do in this moment."

"Oh!" Violet said, glancing over his shoulder. "I didn't realize."

He smiled a little. "I've rubbed off on you, Duchess. A month ago, you would have lectured me about keeping the door open for propriety's sake."

"I've rubbed off on you too," she pointed out. "A month ago, you'd have boinked me against the wall with the door open, without any care for gossip."

His mouth tilted upward on one side. "Boinked?"

"Ashley's word."

He nodded in acknowledgment, though his smile had already started to fade. "What are you doing here? You've never come by the office before."

"I wanted to see how the interviews went," she said, a bit too brightly, making the lie almost painfully transparent even to her own ears.

He merely gazed at her.

"No," she said, with a sigh. "That's not true. I mean, I *did* want to know how they went, but it isn't why I came downtown."

Cain stayed still. Waited.

Violet took a deep breath. "Cain, before the vote, before the Heart Ball on Saturday, before you're named CEO—"

"We don't know that I will be."

"You will," she said with quiet confidence. "You're incredible, Cain. Not because of the suit, or the hair, or because you know what an amuse-bouche is now, or the difference between Monet and Manet. You're smart, and kind, even though you try to hide it, and . . ." She inhaled. "Those are the reasons why I lo—"

"Don't." His voice was rough. "Please don't."

"But—"

His dark eyes were pleading. "Duchess, if you care for me even a little bit, please don't say those words."

Violet felt her heart breaking. "But *why?*"

"Because you'll make what I need to do impossible," he said before turning and walking out of the room.

Twenty-Seven

Violet stared at her reflection in the Met's bathroom. She had never felt so glamorous on the outside and so dead on the inside.

"What do you think he meant, *impossible?*" Ashley asked as she reapplied red lipstick that perfectly matched her red dress. "What could he *need* to do?"

"I have no idea," Violet said, biting her tongue to keep from adding *for the hundredth time.*

They'd been over the conversation ad nauseum, and she was no closer to understanding Cain's odd behavior than Ashley was. Adding to the strangeness of the befuddling encounter was that even *Edith* was avoiding her. Violet had expected to hear something from someone following the vote yesterday afternoon, but Alvin had told her Edith was swamped with last-minute details for the gala and the big announcement.

Violet was too proud to reach out to Cain directly, especially after he'd left her standing alone in his office like some sort of rejected old toy he no longer had a use for.

"Does it cheer you up at all to know that he's been looking at you all night?" Ashley asked, turning to Violet and reaching out to smooth a flyaway hair.

Violet had picked out the dress just days ago, forgoing the typical pink or red Valentine's theme she'd originally planned on, and opting for a vivid purple.

Violet, the tag had read. Violets had been her mother's favorite flower, hence the name, and she'd frequently dressed her only daughter in her namesake color. Violet had avoided the shade entirely since her parents' death. Not intentionally; it had just somehow seemed too bold, too bright for the version of herself she'd so carefully cultivated.

Now, even through her anger at Cain—perhaps because of it—the color felt right. The dress was simple in cut. Floor length, but with a deep slit up to midthigh. A modest neckline to complement her ever-present pearls, but a flirty low back.

She'd let Ashley do her hair. A simple chignon at the back of her head, to show off the diamond and pearl cluster earrings Edith had sent over via Alvin, and Violet hadn't felt quite peeved enough at the other woman to snub the gesture.

A harried-looking woman who worked for Edith entered

the restroom and did a double take when she saw Violet. "Violet! You should be out there. They're about to announce the new CEO!"

"We were just leaving," Ashley said with a smile, dropping her lip gloss into her clutch and pulling Violet's arm to the door.

"Do we have to?" Violet muttered under her breath.

"Yes," her friend said firmly.

"I feel like I'm going to puke."

"If you're nervous, think how Cain must be feeling. He needs you, sweetie. I know it doesn't feel like he does, I know he's been a turd pile, but trust me on this. I've been watching him watch you all night. You're his life preserver."

It was just about the only thing that could have gotten Violet to step into the crowded ballroom. Dan Bogan was already at the microphone, delivering a boring welcome speech as Violet let Ashley weave her through the crowd until they were in the first couple of rows in front of the stage.

She felt rather than saw Cain up on the stage. She'd sensed his presence all night, though this was the first time she'd let herself look his way.

Violet expected him to be ignoring her, but her stomach dropped when she found him looking right at her. His gaze was dark and piercing, as unreadable as it had been that first day in Edith's parlor. She had no idea what he was thinking, what he was feeling . . .

A quick glance at Edith didn't give Violet any more information. The woman had always had a frustratingly impressive poker face.

The rest of the board members looked equally impassive. Only Keith wore any expression at all, one Violet could only describe as smug.

Oh dear.

"Keith's smirk is not a good sign," Ashley murmured, echoing Violet's thoughts.

Keith had made no effort to hide his opposition to Cain as CEO. If he was looking this happy . . .

Violet's heart began to hammer, and not in a good way.

Dan was in the process of handing over the microphone to Edith, who was dressed in a stunning maroon gown paired with the ruby necklace Bernard had given her for their fortieth wedding anniversary.

"I'll start by echoing Dan's gratitude for you all joining us tonight. My late husband was always a hopeless romantic, and Valentine's Day was his favorite holiday—when he proposed. When we got married."

Edith dabbed her eyes before continuing. "I always miss him most on February fourteenth, but this year in particular is bittersweet, as I know he'd have wanted to be here to see Rhodes off to its next stage, with such a bright future ahead."

She cleared her throat. "Some of you may know that this is my final year as the head of the company. It's been a vital part of my life for so long, and it's not a decision I've made easily. But it's time to let the next generation take over so I can finally pursue my life's desire: drinking gin and tonics at noon."

Edith waited until the laughter faded before continuing. "The search for the next CEO has been a slow, deliberate one, as I know I speak for everyone on this stage when I say we've wanted to find the right fit. We're still not quite there, but we have found someone perfectly suited to fill the position while we continue our search."

Wait, whaaaaaat?

Edith smiled brightly, shifting the microphone from one hand to the other, and Violet thought she saw her hand shake just a little. "And so, on behalf of myself and the entire Rhodes International leadership team, I'd like to congratulate our new acting CEO: Mr. Keith Schultz."

Violet didn't move a single muscle as all the blood seemed to drain from her face. In fact, she felt completely boneless as she stood there, frozen, trying to figure out if she'd just heard what she'd thought she'd heard.

"Keith?" Ashley said, echoing Violet's disbelief. Luckily her added *eww* was drowned out by the applause from the rest of the room as a beaming Keith walked across the stage, taking the microphone from Edith.

Violet spared him only the briefest of glances before looking at a wooden Cain, who stood as still as Violet herself.

He'd known, she realized. She couldn't tell exactly what he was feeling, but she knew it wasn't surprise.

What the hell had happened?

She turned her attention back to Keith, wanting to demand he justify his presence, to explain this turn of events. But he was too busy going on and on about the great honor, his grand vision . . .

"I did have one small regret upon learning the news, however," Keith was saying. "I've been privy to the fact that Edith's and Bernard's fondest wish was to keep the company in the family."

Violet glanced again at Cain, and this time she saw the faintest of flinches. Edith's was less subtle.

Keith was still wearing his smarmy smile. "Some of you may know that in addition to being blessed with the discovery of Mr. Stone here, Edith has had a surrogate granddaughter the past few years, a woman she's told me herself she loves as much as her own flesh and blood."

Violet looked in surprise at Edith, who smiled back with a slight nod.

"Violet, would you join me up here for a moment?" Keith asked, and she noticed he had to scan the crowd for her.

Cain, on the other hand, had immediately known where she was.

"Gross," Ashley was muttering. "But you have to get up there, sweetie."

Violet let her friend gently nudge her toward the stairs at the side of the stage, though it wasn't Ashley who helped her navigate up the steps on shaky legs, nor was it Keith.

It was Cain. He extended a hand, which Violet took without hesitation, holding his dark gaze as she made her way up the steps.

For an awful, heartbreaking moment, she could read him. And he looked *tortured.*

"Wonderful, wonderful," Keith was saying, shooing the other board members out of Violet's way. Only when Keith reached for her other hand, did Violet tear her eyes away from Cain's.

His fingers tightened for a fraction of a second, as though not wanting to let her go, then he dropped her hand and his mask back into place.

Keith pulled her forward again, until she was forced to stand center stage with him, all eyes on her.

"I can't magically make Rhodes blood flow through my veins to keep the company in the family," Keith said, with a laugh at his own "joke," "but I can do the next best thing. Edith, if you'd hold this a moment, please," he said, handing her the microphone.

Before Violet could comprehend what he was doing, Keith dropped to his knee and pulled a velvet box out of the inner pocket of his tux jacket.

The crowd gasped in delight. Violet gasped in horror. Wide-eyed, her gaze cut to her right to see an equally aghast Ashley standing there with her hand over her chest.

Violet could read Ashley's lips. "He wouldn't."

They were about to find out he would.

"Violet, my love," Keith said, dragging Violet's stunned attention back to him.

My love? *Since when?*

"For the past several years, you've been my rock. My companion. My best friend. I didn't realize until recently just how lost I am without you, didn't fully comprehend that what I felt for you wasn't just gratitude, or affection, but it was, in fact, the sort of undying love that only comes around once in a lifetime. As I start this new journey in my professional life, it seems only fitting that I begin a new personal journey as well. Will you do me the honor of becoming my wife and keeping this great company in the family?"

Oh. My. God.

Of all the underhanded, slimy, manipulative . . .

"Darling?" Keith prompted, his face adoring as he looked up at her.

Everyone was looking at her, she realized in horror. It was quite possibly her nightmare proposal. The setting was wrong, the timing was wrong, the audience was wrong, the *man* was wrong.

But he was a man. A man she wouldn't humiliate in front of everyone. Not because she was perfect, people-pleasing Violet. Not because she was a placid paper doll who did others' bidding. But because even an opportunistic man like Keith deserved to be rejected in private.

Because Violet Townsend knew the person she was: kind.

So she forced a smile. She couldn't bring herself to say yes; she wouldn't lie. But she let him push the ring on her finger, even as she began rehearsing the gentle letdown speech she would deliver shortly after.

Violet let herself be swept into a sea of congratulations, which she merely smiled at, knowing it would translate as stunned shyness.

She caught the scent of Edith's familiar Lancôme perfume a moment before the older woman flanked her on one side. Smelled Ashley's more citrusy perfume on the other, as Ashley protected her from the other side.

And she felt immediate relief, knowing they knew. Knowing they would support her.

Fittingly, the one least clued in to her distress seemed to be Keith, who was happily accepting the congrats on his promotion and his engagement, though he hadn't so much as glanced at Violet since putting the ring on her finger.

Violet didn't care. She wasn't looking at him either. She was searching the crowd for another man entirely but couldn't find him.

"Cain," Violet whispered to Ashley. "Can you get me to Cain?"

Her friend squeezed her hand tightly. "I'm so sorry, sweetie. He left the second that idiot got down on one knee."

Twenty-Eight

"What did he say when you gave the ring back?" Alvin asked, pushing a cup of tea into Violet's hand.

Edith was sitting beside Violet and pushed the teacup right back into Alvin's hands. "For God's sake Alvin, get the girl some brandy."

"Brandy?" Ashley said in surprise.

"Something boozy. *Anything*," Edith said with a wave of her hand.

Ashley pursed her lips, then scooped up Coco and gestured for Alvin to follow her out of Edith's parlor. "Come on, Al. Let's go see if you guys have got any tequila."

"Slow down, young lady. I can't walk as quick as I could, what with this flesh-eating bacteria on my tibia."

Violet glanced at Edith for context.

"He scraped his shin on the brick wall in the garden,"

Edith murmured. "I put the Neosporin on it myself. He's fine."

"Ah," Violet said with a forced smile as she bowed her head tiredly.

"Oh, Violet," Edith said, taking her hand. "You've had quite a night."

"And you too," Violet said, looking up to meet Edith's eyes. "What happened, Edith? How could the board not see how smart Cain was, how much he wanted it, how great—"

"They did."

Violet blinked. "What?"

"The board approved Cain in the vote yesterday. Not unanimously—I think we can assume you-know-who voted for himself. But there was overwhelming confidence in Cain's abilities."

"Then why . . ."

Edith touched her ruby necklace with a puzzlingly happy smile on her face. "Cain came to me yesterday morning. After the vote, but before the results. He let me know he didn't want it."

Violet's heart sank and broke at the same time. "He's going back to his life in New Orleans," she said flatly.

"No, no. I should have clarified," Edith said quickly. "He said he didn't want it *like this*. He didn't want a job because it had been handed to him by circumstance of his birth. He wants to be CEO of the company someday, but he wants to do it the right way. To work his way to the top. He wants to *earn* it."

The news should have felt like a bombshell, but it somehow . . . didn't. It fit. Cain, who so desperately wanted to be seen and appreciated for who he was, wouldn't have been proud to take over the company simply because he'd shaved.

"You're okay with this?" Violet asked Edith.

"More than okay. I could not be prouder, in fact, and I have no doubt he'll climb the ladder in record time so we can oust that—that . . . *douche* from my office," Edith said with a fierce scowl.

Violet smiled a little at Edith's unexpected use of the word *douche*, but her heart wasn't in it.

"Why didn't Cain just tell me?" she asked Edith miserably.

Edith's smile faded. "He begged me not to tell you and wouldn't tell me why, though . . . I do have some suspicions."

Violet waited.

"I think," Edith said, choosing her words carefully, "that a man who wants to earn a job the right way would want to earn a woman's love the right way too."

"But love isn't earned," Violet protested. "It's given. Freely."

Edith smiled fondly and tucked Violet's hair behind her ear. "I'm happy to hear you say that. And I hope you know that you've never had to earn my love."

"Let's just say it's been a recent realization," Violet said. "But I appreciate hearing it. Oh, and Edith, while we're on the topic of employment—"

"You're going to quit working for me for free? It's about damn time. I would have fired you for your own good had you not said something." Edith patted her knee as Ashley and Alvin came back into the room, this time Alvin carrying Coco, who was dressed in a pink diamond sweater, and Ashley carrying the tray.

"Are those my cordial glasses?" Edith asked, putting on her glasses to see the tray more clearly. "I haven't used those in ages."

"No cordial tonight, Edith. Tonight, we celebrate Valentine's Day the only way four single people should: with Patrón," Ashley said, handing around the makeshift shot glasses.

"And thank goodness for that," Alvin said, dropping into the chair and setting down a squirming Coco, who raced over to snuggle between Edith and Violet. "I don't know what bothered me more, Violet, the split second of worrying you might actually marry Keith, or learning he was CEO."

"*Acting* CEO," Edith reminded them quickly.

"Yeah, I noticed Keith liked to skip over that clarification," Ashley added with an eye roll. "Regardless, sweetie, it was kind of you to not humiliate him in front of a crowd. I don't know that I'd have had the stomach to do the same."

"It felt like the right thing at the time," Violet said, absently petting her dog. "But . . ."

"Cain?" Ashley asked softly.

Violet squeezed her eyes shut. "I hate that *he* thinks I'm

engaged. But I think I hate even more that he might not care."

"Oh, he cares," Edith said with confidence. "But you're not going to remedy anything sitting on that young butt of yours."

"Edith, if you had any idea how often your grandson has rejected me . . ."

"Yes, but those times were different," Edith said firmly.

"How so?" Ashley asked, looking as puzzled as Violet by Edith's conviction.

"Because," Edith said smugly, "today is Valentine's Day."

An hour later, standing outside Cain's door, Violet felt the liquid courage from the tequila fade just as quickly as her faith in Cupid.

She'd been knocking for ten minutes, taken a break on the off chance he was in the shower and couldn't hear her, then knocked some more.

The other side of the door remained stubbornly silent, the door itself remained heartbreakingly closed.

Cain either wasn't home or was giving her a very pointed message.

Tired, frustrated, and missing him, Violet gave his door the tiniest kick with the tip of her stiletto, then uttered Cain Stone's very favorite word that started with an F.

Twenty-Nine

As Violet let herself back into her dark apartment, she regretted leaving Coco with Alvin and Edith for the night. She'd been hoping to have an adult slumber party at Cain's house.

But now she was simply alone.

Violet tossed her clutch onto the kitchen table and poured herself a glass of water. She drained it, then kicking off her shoes, began the process of pulling the pins out of her hair as she made her way to the living room.

The evening called for the most melancholy jazz in her collection, no "My Funny Valentine" or any mention of love allowed.

Violet switched on the side table lamp and then let out a startled scream when she saw the man sitting on the couch.

"*Cain?*"

"Hey, Duchess," he said, leaning forward slightly, his hands clasped loosely between his knees. He was still wearing his tux, but the bow tie dangled around his neck, and his jaw was shadowed.

"What . . ." She placed a hand over her galloping heart. "How the hell did you get in here?"

He held up a key. "Found it in Adam's things the first day I got to New York."

"And you thought *tonight* was the best night to use it?" she asked incredulously.

"Actually, yes."

Realizing her heart was beating fast for reasons other than being startled, Violet made her way to her records and began flipping through them as a way of settling her nerves, or at least disguising them.

"You've got an impressive collection," he said from behind her.

"You snooped?"

"Of course."

Violet said nothing for a moment as she selected an Oscar Peterson record that had been one of her father's favorites.

She moved to the record player and put the vinyl on, letting the skilled pianist fill the awkward silence in the room.

"I didn't expect you home so late."

Violet watched the record spin but said nothing.

"Actually, that's not true. I guess I didn't expect you home at all. Figured you'd be celebrating your engagement."

The casual indifference in his tone, as though it didn't matter to him one way or another, brought tears to her eyes. Edith had been wrong. There *was* no magic on Valentine's Day, Cain didn't feel the same way. She *wasn't* meant to be loved just as she was—

"Don't do it, Duchess." His voice was closer now. Rougher. "Please don't marry him. Please, *Violet*."

Violet's head snapped up and she turned around, finding Cain just a few inches away, wearing that same tortured expression she'd seen on the stage, his hands shoved into his pockets.

"I told myself to let you go," he said. "When I decided I couldn't accept the CEO position this way, I told myself you deserved better than a guy just starting his career over from scratch. You deserve the guy at the top, the guy with the jet, the champagne, the yacht . . . You deserve the best. And so I was going to step aside, give you back the life you had before I came in and ruined everything."

"You didn't ruin everything," Violet whispered.

Cain moved cautiously closer. "No?"

Silently, Violet lifted her left hand. Her unadorned left hand.

Cain stared at it a moment, then looked back at her. "You said no."

"I said no."

"Because Keith's a tool?"

She smiled. "That. And other reasons."

"What other reasons?"

Her heart crumpled a little at the memory of his office. "You told me not to say. That you couldn't bear it."

"I was wrong," he said roughly. "I realized tonight that not hearing it is what I won't be able to bear. Please," he said, his voice pleading, sliding a hand to the back of her neck. "Please."

"I love you," Violet whispered.

His eyes squeezed shut.

"I lied, you know," Cain said gruffly, rubbing his thumbs along her jaw tenderly. "When I told you I didn't want the wife, the kids, the picnics in Central Park."

"You did?"

He nodded. "I *do* love picnics."

Violet punched his chest, and he laughed and pulled her closer. His laugh faded as he rested his forehead on hers. "I lied because I only ever wanted those things after I met you. And I was . . ." Cain swallowed. "I thought maybe if I could talk myself out of wanting all that, it wouldn't hurt so much if you didn't want them with me."

"Cain." Violet placed her hand on his cheek. "I want them with you. But . . . your life in New Orleans. Your work, your apartment . . ."

"Will always be important to me," Cain said. "But as a part of my past. I love New Orleans, and I'll go back when-

ever I can. But to visit. Not stay. I'm ready for a new challenge. A new life. Maybe . . ." He cleared his throat. "A new
wife?"

Violet wrapped her fingers around each side of his tie.
"Does this mean you're my guy after all?" she teased.

His eyes closed, then he inhaled a deep breath. When he
opened his eyes again, they looked shinier than before.
"Damn it, Duchess. I am so in love with you. Yeah. Hell
yeah, I'm your guy."

Violet lifted to her toes to brush her lips over his. "I sure
as hell hope so. Because I'm going to be your girl for the rest
of my life."

Epilogue

"Daddy! My turn, my turn!"

"It most certainly is *not* your turn," Cain said from the piano bench, scooping up three-year-old Marla onto his knee. "It's Emily's turn to play. But I appreciate your bullish negotiating skills. You take after Great-Grandma."

"Don't flatter the girl with compliments, Cain. It'll go straight to her head," Edith said, as she entered the parlor armed with cookies and lemonade. "Emily, love, that's wonderful. You play better every time I hear you."

"That's because she prax-tixed," Marla said around a mouthful of cookie.

"And Marla doesn't," Emily said with big-sister superiority.

"You didn't practice much when you were her age either, sweetheart," Violet said, bending to kiss the top of Emily's head. She caught Cain's eyes over their daughter's dark ponytail and felt her stomach flip when he smiled at her.

Several years married, and she still got butterflies around the man.

The moment was interrupted by two-year-old Dandelion, a clumsy golden retriever that rammed into the back of Violet's knees while being chased by a gleefully barking Coco, who was rocking the hell out of her old age.

It wasn't a peaceful existence, but it was a happy one that had exceeded Violet's expectations on every level.

"I didn't miss presents yet, did I?"

"Presents!" Emily screamed, whirling away from the piano and remembering the reason they were all there—her birthday. "Did you get me something, Great-Grandpa?"

"Of course, I did, sweetheart. You like turnips, right?"

Edith had met Joe Kaplan at a social club for single people struggling to settle into retired life, and they'd married just a few months after they began dating. As Edith had pragmatically pointed out, at her age, there was no time to waste.

Violet and Cain were thrilled for them, but nobody was perhaps quite as happy as Alvin. Joe was a retired physician, which meant Alvin had access to a doctor who was all too happy to keep his medical training alive and well for all of Alvin's ailments.

Edith had found a way to ease into retirement as well. Cain had asked her to be his official mentor, an arrangement that had not only given their relationship a chance to blossom, but had resulted in Cain being voted in as CEO—unanimously—just a year after the first vote. Keith had been *encouraged* to resign after it had quickly become clear he was far more interested in the label of CEO than he was in the job itself.

"Cain, some champagne?" Edith asked, holding up a bottle.

"Of course. Gotta celebrate the birthday girl," he said as Emily climbed onto his lap, Coco clutched in her arms, wearing a DIVA sweater. "Thanks, Grandma," he said, accepting the glass.

Emily picked up one of the wrapped gifts and gave it a shake before checking the tag. She beamed up at Cain. "This one's from you, Daddy."

"Sure is."

Emily looked thoughtfully over at Violet, who was rubbing her very pregnant stomach—their first boy, due in two months.

"Mommy?" Emily said. "Does Daddy ever get you birthday presents?"

"Of course. You saw me open them in May," Violet said, nibbling a cookie.

"Oh. That's right. What was the first present he *ever* got you?"

"The first? Piano lessons."

"Piano lessons! For your birthday?"

"Actually, no. It was the day after Valentine's Day."

"Why the day *after* Valentine's Day, Daddy?"

"Because we were busy on that particular day," he said, rubbing his bearded chin affectionately on the top of his daughter's head. "But I bought the gift a long time before that."

"When?"

"The first time I ever heard her play 'Heart and Soul.'"

"Why did you buy her lessons then?" Marla chimed in. "Was she bad?"

"No. No." Cain met Violet's eyes across the room. "Because I knew even then that I loved her."

Author's Note

There are some book ideas that seem to have been rattling around in my brain forever, little seeds of a story that the Muse presents year after year, as if to say, "*Now* are you ready to write this one?"

The premise of *Made in Manhattan* was exactly that kind of story. I'd been fascinated with *Pygmalion* ever since reading George Bernard Shaw's iconic play my sophomore year of high school—an obsession that became even more firmly cemented by the nearly simultaneous release of the *Pygmalion*-inspired movie *She's All That*.

In fact, the premise of a man "changing" a woman, only to fall for the real her, made it into one of my earliest published books (*Isn't She Lovely*), which remains both one of my bestsellers and personal favorite.

But apparently the Muse wasn't done with *Pygmalion*. It

begged to do another version, an even fresher spin with a woman making over a man. In other words, the idea for *Made in Manhattan* feels as though it's been around forever, and yet . . .

My goodness, it was not as easy to write as I'd anticipated. Violet and Cain were unusual characters for me in that as I was writing, they *refused* to adhere to my outline. Instead of the tidy opposites-attract romance I'd envisioned, it turned into something far more complex.

It became a story not so much of a woman "making over" a man, but instead the journey of two flawed, complicated individuals who *desperately* want to be loved but who have to kill a few demons to get there. It's a story about discovering that we all deserve to be loved *just as we are.*

The result was an almost startlingly rewarding writing experience, and one that I absolutely could not have undertaken alone. I cannot stress enough how much my editor, the incredible Sara Quaranta, helped with this story. In its earliest stages, when I felt like I just couldn't *crack the damn thing,* I unloaded my rambling thoughts on Sara, who came back with one single insight that completely unlocked the romance for me. Lightbulb moments like that are rare and wonderful, something only an amazing editor like Sara can gift an author. I'm beyond grateful.

And then there's the almost impossibly patient Molly Gregory, to whom I am most grateful for her unwavering support and encouragement, and her commitment to helping me make this the best book possible.

I'm grateful, as always, to my agent Nicole Resciniti, not only for her constant wisdom and championing of my career but also for a most incredible friendship. I am counting the days until we can drink Manhattans together in person instead of over Zoom!

To the entire team at Gallery, you guys are absolutely exceptional. Christine Masters, I won't lie, I sort of want to *be* you, though I wouldn't do it nearly as well. You are, as far as I'm concerned, a magician. For the entire editing, marketing, and publicity teams, as well as all the behind-the-scenes stuff I don't even *know* about, I'm in constant awe and gratitude for your ability to turn my messy idea into a beautiful finished project.

My friends and family, I love you guys. Anth, especially, thank you for bringing me scrambled eggs every single morning in bed, and not judging me for inhaling them while bent over my laptop, writing Cain and Violet's story.

Lastly, to you who's reading this right now, it likely means that you've just finished Cain and Violet's story, and I'm honored you trusted me with your precious reading time.

Sometimes it doesn't feel quite real that this is my life: writing love stories for a living, that people actually read. I'm beyond grateful for everyone who's made that possible.

Thank you,
Lauren Layne